SURVIVAL
OF THE
UNTHINKABLE

by

FRED HAMLIN

Vabella Publishing
P.O. Box 1052
Carrollton, Georgia 30112
www.vabella.com

This book has no connection, relationship, or affiliation with the 2010 motion picture *Unthinkable*.

Cover image is public domain.
Images on pages 8-11 from *Family Shelter Series*.
Image on page 22 is public domain.

13-digit ISBN 978-1-942766-17-9

Library of Congress Control Number 2016909937

10 9 8 7 6 5 4 3 2 1

I am dedicating this book to my loving wife Sharon Hamlin. We have been married to for forty-nine years. While writing this, I came down with advanced stage four cancer of the throat. Sharon has never stopped believing in me or looking after me. She also did a fine job editing my book and contributing to its quality.

Acknowledgments

Thanks to the Carroll County Writers Club in Carrollton, Georgia, USA. They meet the 2nd and 4th Tuesday of every month. They also meet on the 3rd Saturday of the month and on Wednesdays for Poetry. Time is at 10 AM for each meeting. They meet in the Cultural Arts Center in Carrollton, Georgia. The members each listened and help fine tune my novel.

CCWC members and Vabella Publishing of Carrollton, Georgia, USA, after hearing what I was writing about encouraged me to finish.

So, as not to offend anyone by accidently leaving a name off, I won't list names of the people who encouraged me to do this, and I heartedly say thank you to all that knew about the writing of this novel. Thank you very much.

Characters

James Cummings - a forty year old man trained as a radiological specialist by the Federal Emergency Management Association for the southeast region of the United States.

Judy Cummings - thirty five year old wife of James Cumming who is raising Bill and Catherine their two children.

Bill Cummings - twelve year old son of James and Judy.

Catherine Cummings - ten year old daughter of James and Judy.

David McDaniel - truck driver who lost his job. (Found gold)

Sara McDaniel - young wife of David McDaniel.

Tim Guard - electronics specialist trained by the US Navy.

Dr. Ralph Vickers - general physician.

Martha Vickers - wife of Dr. Vickers.

Dr. Rogers - dentist from West Georgia Area.

Betty Goodbye - girl friend of Dr. Rogers.

Greg Potter - Officer in Charge in Marines

Andy Wallace - Medical Officer in Marines

Sharon Green - Amish

Betty Anderson - accident victim

Old man and old woman shot and killed at old worn out hardware store

Eight mean men killed and horses taken

Three extra women by tree

SURVIVAL
OF THE
UNTHINKABLE

Chapter One

"Get up, get up, please get up, James!" Judy said.

"What in the world is the matter?" James asked.

"The World News's just reported 10 Soviet SS-10 ICBM missiles are moving over the polar cap, toward the United States, you told me this could happen any time, and I guess you are right." Judy said.

"Get the children quick, we have to leave now," James instructed.

"I do not want to leave our home James, everything we love and cherish is right here," his wife Judy stated. James looks at Judy's face drawn and tired, for a thirty five year old mother of two.

"It's almost three o' clock in the afternoon, now get Bill and Catherine and please do not upset them; you know they are still only ten and twelve years old." Judy went outside to call for the kids. The sky looked clear with a few fluffy clouds drifting lazily by. James went down stairs to gather the emergency bags that were packed away many months ago, and then he stopped and thought, I'm forty years old, why is this happening to my family now, when we have everything to live for.

"Daddy have we got to leave now, Catherine and I are having so much fun outside?"

"Bill, help me get all these bags in the truck so we can move to the shelter quickly." James said.

"Everybody in the truck, we are leaving! Is everybody comfortable, with everything we have piled in with us?" Judy hollered.

"We just about don't have enough room," Bill said.

"Everything we have in the truck is necessary, I just wish we could have put more in the truck and still get to the shelter in time," James said.

"I know we must have spent at least fifteen or twenty minutes just getting packed and in the truck, how far to the shelter James?" Judy asks.

"About twenty miles and we have to be there before the first missile touches down. Where do you think it will hit James?" Judy asked looking very worried.

"Atlanta, Georgia is a big area Judy, and that is why one SS-10 missile carries ten reentry war heads each able to target independently and accurately. Hartsfield Jackson International Airport and Dobbins Air Force Base surely will be two high priority targets. The prevailing winds are mostly easterly and that is why we bought our home at least fifty miles west of Atlanta fourteen years ago," James said.

"Daddy the traffic is getting really bad, everybody is leaving Atlanta I think," Bill stated.

"Look at all the people walking daddy, and they are all going the same way we are, can we carry some of them?" Catherine asked.

"Do you want them to sit in your lap?" Judy questioned her daughter.

"I don't think so." Catherine said.

"Don't slow down any more James; I'm getting nervous with all these people walking beside the truck." Judy said.

James turned around in the seat, looked real hard at his two children, and said, "Lock your car doors."

"Daddy, there's a woman in the back of the truck." Bill screamed. James looked in the rear view mirror and saw the woman, sitting in the hot sun, completely exhausted.

"Pull over James and find out what's going on." Judy stated.

James slowly pulled into the grass and got out. "What is your name young lady?"

"My name is Sara and I can't walk any further."

"Sara, what is your last name?" James asks.

"Sara McDaniel, this is my husband David McDaniel," Sara said, looking pale, tired, and worn out holding his hand and squeezing hard while looking him in the eyes. "My husband and I just want to get away, as soon as we can."

"David, I'm James Cummings and we do not have much time, get in the truck, next to your wife."

"Where are we going James?" David questioned.

"West, as fast as we can, Sara you and your husband will be safe, I promise." James said. "We have to be at the shelter in at least twenty minutes." James was watching Sara and David in the mirror with the strong summer wind blowing through their hair. "We are making better time now that the crowd has thinned out, and should be there in just a minute." James stated. James pulled off the road going through some heavy brush.

David hollered, "This is not a road at all." Just two hundred feet ahead, was a huge hill going straight up with brush and small trees all around.

"We're here," James hollered. "Everyone get out of the truck, and let's empty the truck, so I can hide the truck. Take a long look around and remember what you see."

"Where are we, there's nothing here?" Sara asks.

"Oh yes there is," Judy said, "look over to the right." As they turned, a huge locked door appeared.

"I never saw it," David commented, "and it was right in front of us."

James stood up straight and said to everyone; "I won't all of you to look around and enjoy the clear sky, the beautiful trees, and the smell of fresh air. You won't be enjoying these things you've taken for granted, in the next few months." Now that everyone had gotten out of the truck, James drove the truck into a metal building painted green and brown with a large sliding door. Then James got out and closed the sliding door by hand. "Listen up everyone that metal building will protect the electrical equipment in the pickup truck from EMP electromagnetic pulse. This building in the atomic world is termed a faraday shield and the entire building is grounded with metal stakes into the ground. Now, let's get that door open to the shelter," James ordered. James pulled out a big key in which would open the door of the shelter. "Seven minutes left!" Judy hollered. With that, James inserted the key and tried to turn it. "Oh no, do not tell me it won't open."

About that time David hollered, "Move out of the way," and he brought down a ten -pound sledgehammer right on the top of the lock. The sound was devastating and startled everyone. The lock exploded into two pieces.

"David, I am glad you are part of our group today," Judy commented.

"Before we go in I have to say something, from now on, your living conditions as you know it will never be the same as long as you are in this shelter and even after you come out," James stated.

"We are already fifteen minutes late getting in the shelter," Judy stated, as James began pulling on the door.

David then hollered, "Get out of my way." David began swinging the sledgehammer hard and hit the steel hinges solid.

"Not again," James hollered, "that sledge will not move that five hundred pound blue steel plate door with cast iron hinges. Get the grease and pump some grease in that nipple to lubricate the hinges." Judy was already doing just that as she had been taught a year ago and Sara was helping her, "that's what I call team work," James said. Bill was pulling again on the massive steel door, "someone give me some help, he hollered," and the door began to open. Before anyone could move, an unbelievable bright light was burning itself against the door coming from an easterly location. James with his sweating face, drawn in eyes and understandable exhausted body said, "We are out of time. I was hoping it would not come to this." Everyone gave James a depressed look. James, looking at everyone's tired face said, "Let's go in, and grab some bags on the way in."

Catherine hollered, "I'm scared, it's dark in there."

"I'll light some oil lamps in just a minute. Turn on your flashlights and hold my hand as we go in," James said.

"Are we ready to close the door now?" Judy asks.

"Yes, let's all work together." James commented. Everyone pulled as hard as they could and the massive door closed slowly.

"I've never seen it so dark before," Sara stated, while shivering from the cold, now settling on her sweaty face.

"It will stay a constant fifty four degrees even in the winter and summer, year round," James told everyone. James with his light still on was turning on a small LED light close by. A very small light came on.

"We've got trouble!" James indicated. "The batteries are not charged up as they should be."

"Your right, we only have eight volts charged in the battery pack," Judy replies while looking at the gauges.

"What do we do?" David asks.

"I will have to go outside and clean the leaves off of the solar panels that are responsible for charging the deep cycle, twelve volt battery pack. At a cost of three thousand dollars, they need to be clean, don't you think? I need water," James said, walking with his flashlight to the back of the cave. "This is where we get water," pointing to the rock wall, shining with tumbling water on the side of the limestone face. After collecting around two gallons of water in a bucket, Judy turned and handed the bucket to James and said, "Please hurry." James grabbed the bucket to wash the solar panels on top of the hill free of trash and started to run toward the door.

"Get ready to open the door while I put on this protective suit to protect me against radiation. I'll be back in just a second." Everybody started pulling on the huge door, hoping it would start to open. James shouted; "pull that big leaver to unlock the pins."

With both hands, Bill and David pulled straight down and all the eight pins moved at once. James knew he did not have much time before the radiation level would be too high for him to go outside at all, but he had too, because he had forgotten to clean the solar panels before everyone went inside. The door slowly opened and James ran quickly out, and up the hill. There high on that hill, were those magnificent panels that with the help of his brother in-law, Tim Guard, they installed about a year ago. Tim was an electronics specialist trained by our armed forces, the U. S. Navy. James flushed the solar panels with water and wiped them down. It is so pretty outside James thought; it is a shame to have to go back inside. Sliding carefully down the hill James came to the steel door and started to bang on it. Gradually the door opened slowly and James ran into the dark shelter. Being hot and tired, James sat down to get his breath for a few minutes in the cool fifty-four degree air, cooling his face. Everyone was sitting facing James waiting; it seemed like forever, for him to give him or her some kind of support. With oil lamps lit, James spoke to all of those in the small circle.

"I would like to go over a few things with everyone, so you might understand what is at stake here and now. In addition, what each of you will need to do in the near future, in order to make this shelter work. This cave was turned into a shelter in this location for me to monitor the radiation strength levels in the area and to be transmitted to Mission Control in Atlanta, so they can notify the Federal Emergency Management Agency in Washington. D.C. Therefore, they will then know which locations are considered too high in radiation to move troops through. I will take readings of the radiation once a day for this purpose, while protecting as many citizens of the community as possible and give medical care along with protection from outside elements if necessary. Others will be joining us in a few hours I hope. David, are you familiar with how to build a small shelter at your home?"

"Are you kidding, I never thought or let alone dreamed I would need a shelter and did not know such material existed until just now." David answered in surprise.

"Bill, get the manual on the shelf by you and give to David and Sara to look over."

"Okay dad. Here, Mr. McDaniel."

"Bill, since we are going to be in here a while you and Catherine might as well call my wife, and I by our first names, David and Sara."

"David these shelters are reasonable to build for three or four people but are too small to hold enough food and water for a long time. Some do not have room for a decontamination station or a medical room. Look thru these pages and you will see what I am talking about."

SHELTER SUPPLIES CHECKLIST

Food and cooking equipment:
Water (2-week supply, a minimum of 7 gal. per person)
Food (2-week supply)
Eating utensils
Paper plates, cups and napkins (2-week supply)
Openers for cans and bottles
Pocket knife
Special foods for babies and the sick

Supplies and equipment for sanitation:
Can for garbage (20-gal.)
Covered pail for toilet purposes
Can for human wastes (10-gal.)
Toilet tissue, paper towels, sanitary napkins, disposable diapers, ordinary and waterless soap
Grocery bags, newspapers for soil bags
Household chlorine (2 pt.) and insecticide (1 qt.)
Waterproof gloves

Shelter equipment:
Battery operated radio (AM broadcast) with spare batteries for at least 2-weeks operation
CB radio, shortwave or ham, police scanners are optional but highly desirable
Radiation dosemeter, high level survey meter (500r max. range), and low level radiation meter (geiger counter) for decontamination
Flashlights, electric lantern with spare bulbs and batteries for 2-weeks operation
Clothing
Bedding (special equipment for sick)
First aid medical supplies (special medicines for the sick)
Writing material
Reading material including first aid and other self-help medical books, survival books and titles to help bolster spirits and morale
Tools such as pliers, screwdrivers, etc.
Games and amusements for children

Items outside the shelter but within reach:
Cooking equipment (canned heat, or camp stove) and matches
Home fire-fighting equipment
Rescue tools (shovels, picks, axes, etc.)

77

Image from *Family Shelter Series*

FAMILY SHELTER SERIES   PSD F–61–7

Aboveground Earth-Covered Lumber A-Frame Shelter

GENERAL INFORMATION

The purpose of this shelter is to provide protection for 10 persons from the effects of radioactive fallout at a location near but separate from a residence or other nearby buildings. The principal advantage of this shelter is that it can be erected without excavation in locations where there is poor drainage or where the ground water table is close to the surface. However, this shelter is not a low-cost structure. Footings or thrust ties are needed where the earth is soft or of poor bearing capacity.

TECHNICAL SUMMARY

Space and Occupancy.—This shelter provides almost 150 square feet of area and approximately 640 cubic feet of space. Although only a small portion of this area provides sufficient headroom for standing erect, practically the entire area can serve as sitdown space for 10 persons and storage space for supplies.

23

Image from *Family Shelter Series*

9

SAND FILLED LUMBER LEAN TO
BASEMENT SHELTER

Image from *Family Shelter Series*

PRINCIPLES OF RADIATION DETECTION

METHODS OF DETECTION

Radiations are detected and measured by observing their effects on matter. The basis for detection is ionization. Methods of detection:

Photographic emulsions
Radio Photoluminescence
Scintillation
Chemicals
Enclosed volume of gases

FILM BADGES

Film badges measure the accumulated dose. They are photographic, energy and temperature dependent, and each must be developed. They are not easily calibrated, are not self-reading, have one time use only, and have a short shelf-life.

SURVEY INSTRUMENTS

Survey instruments measure the dose rate.

Ionization Chambers — Small ionization currents are collected from an enclosed chamber of air. An electronic circuit is used to amplify the small currents.

The amplified output current read on a meter is proportional to the current produced by radiation in the ionization chamber. The survey instrument is designed for the meter to read directly in roentgens or milliroentgens per hour.

The range switch changes the amplification of the electronic amplifier.

Ionization chambers are medium and high range survey instruments. They are not the most sensitive type.

HIGH RANGE SURVEY METER
*DCA catalog No. 3010

This survey meter is solid state. Powered by only one "D" size flashlight cell, it will operate for 150 hours under continuous use. Its construction is both rugged and waterproof. RANGE: 0 — 0.5 r/hr, 0 — 5.0 r/hr, 0 — 50.0 r/hr, 0 — 500 r/hr. ENERGY RESPONCE: 60 Kev to 1.5 Mev.

LOW RANGE SURVEY METER
*DCA catalog No. 3007

This solid state survey meter operates with interchangeable probes to monitor alpha, beta and gamma radiation. An ideal meter for decontamination operations. RANGE: 300 cpm, 3000 cpm, 30,000 cpm, 0 — 0.5 mr/hr, 0 — 5 mr/hr, 0 — 50 mr/hr, and with extended range probe the range is extended to read 0 — 500 mr/hr.

Image from *Family Shelter Series*

Chapter Two

It had been a long and trying day. After giving David and Sara a little while to look over the manual and checking over some things, James thought everyone needed to get some rest and unwind.

"Sara, would you and your husband go through some clothes I have over on the other side of the room? Those clothes are various sizes and we need to fit everyone." James requested Sara's help.

"They are all in plastic Zip-bags though," Sara said.

"Plastic zip-bags keep the moisture along with dust and dirt out of the clothing in the shelter," James commented. "When everyone is through with the clothes we will unpack the army cots, with the blankets and line them up over in the corner, it's going to take a day or two for us to get everything set up like it should be," James commented. By this time, everyone's eyes were getting used to the darkened room with the small LED lights placed in key locations all around. Even the small oil lamps placed in the corners help locate your boundaries.

"James," Judy said, "something is wrong with Sara." James looked around to search for her and heard the crying across the cold darkened room. Sara was just visible, sitting on her cot with her head in her hands just sobbing. Her husband was working across the room not seeing his wife in this saddened condition. James and Judy quickly went over, sat on both sides of Sara, and held her for a few minutes until she calmed down "What are we going to do James?"

Judy then spoke up and said, "Sara we are all here to look after you. Why do you think the good Lord put you in our truck on the expressway today for a reason?"

"By the way Sara, I'm going to need a good helper in the medical room and you are going to be busy in the weeks to come," James said.

"You are scaring me now James and I don't want to be." Sara said. James bent over with a big smile and put his arms around Sara, looking at his wife with a smile, and started hugging Sara very playfully.

"As long as we are all here to help, you are going to be just fine and much needed, ok!" James clarified. Everybody was shocked when they heard thunderous banging on the huge steel doors. Judy left Sara sitting and moved quickly in the dimly lit direction of where the pounding was coming from. Everyone was now aware of what Judy was trying to do and was moving in that direction to help her in any way they could. James told everyone not to open that door until he was there, because there could be possible danger on the outside. James was now standing in the middle of the room putting on his protective jump suit with Judy's help.

James then spoke to all of them saying, "Do not to get upset because this is just for precaution, because we do not know the level of radiation outside at this time. Each of you that goes to open the door or in the decontamination area needs to put on the same type of gear. Get your gear on first." James was now putting on his N95 facemask for filtering out all dust partials from the outside and a complete head and eye protector cover. "These people will have to be identified and led through decontamination before they will be allowed to come into this big room with us," James commented to Judy.

Then Judy hollered, "open the door" to everyone standing around! All eight pins on the large steel door started moving as everyone pulled the huge lever together.

"Everybody get back from the door," as it opened about two feet. "Anyone who wants to come inside will have to stand here beside this large rock wall that separates the main room from the decontamination area and get ready to be decontaminated. Dr. Vickers, get yourself in here, I didn't know that was you pounding the door," James abruptly said.

"James, this is my wife Martha, we've only been married for three months now," Dr. Vickers said.

"Martha, move next to your husband by the wall and we will try to get some warm water going so both of you can shower all over. If you or your wife have any accumulated contamination on either of you, it will have to be removed, Dr. Vickers as you already aware."

"Judy, turn on the propane tanks so we can light the burners and heat the hot water tanks for the shower," James asked. As Judy worked with the propane burner, you could see a warm red and yellow glow coming from that general location.

"Dr. Vickers, before you and your wife take your clothes off I need to take a reading with this monitor to determine how much radiation you have picked up while you were traveling." James started using the monitor probe around Dr. Vickers and his wife's arms and legs, to determine if he or his wife were over contaminated. James was still wearing his special jump suit and respirator for protection.

"The water is getting hot!" Judy hollered.

"Dr. Vickers," James said, "you and Martha are way over the safe level according to the monitor, please stay seated behind this rock wall until both of you are decontaminated. The water will be warm enough in about twenty-five or thirty minutes. Dr. Vickers, throw all, I mean, all of your clothes in that large hole in the ground where that yellow colored lid is laying. When you and your wife are through washing with soap and water, I will be checking both of you for any contamination. Make sure your wife washes her hair very good. If she cannot get her hair absolutely clean of contamination we will cut it off."

Dr. Vickers hollered he and his wife were finished washing and had on the large cotton bathrobe's that were furnished. James started using the monitor probe around Dr. Vickers arms and legs first, and then his wife, to determine if he or his wife, Martha were completely decontaminated. Judy noticed Martha starting to shake with the constant cool air in the cave and brought her and her husband some clothing to put on. With the monitor testing negative they were in good shape, even though both of them were tired, dealing with the problems they had encountered.

Bill came over to his mother, Judy, and said "Mom I am hungry."

"I thought you and your sister would be getting hungry by now," Judy said. "Everybody will be eating in a few minutes."

Judy walked over and found Sara talking to her husband, David. "Can your wife help me a few minutes so we can fix everyone something to eat?"

"Yes, please, I am starving, can I help with anything?" David said.

"Both of you come with me and I am going to show you where to find the food stores." Judy said. David and his wife walked slowly in the dimly lit passageway behind Judy, emulated by small LED lights and some oil lamps. Judy reached up on the rough rock wall stopping for just a second and turned a switch on lighting up racks and racks of food stores, lettered and numbered in order to keep an accurate account of inventory. Walking over to a small table Judy picked up a clipboard and found beef stew, under B-23 listed in the pages. "Do you see beef stew under B-23?" Judy asked David and his wife. David nodded "yes."

"I need both of you to go to the proper rack and bring back one large gallon of stew, please?" Judy requested.

"It is way too dark even with the LED lights, to see the cans accurately." Sara said. Judy then pointed to a flashlight on the table by the clipboard and waited quietly as David and Sara disappeared between the long dark racks of food, holding the flashlight.

After a few minutes Judy could see Sara coming back holding the stew over her head, with a big smile on her face as she walked, hollering "it's time to dine at the underground royal palace!" Judy was glad to see Sara in such good spirits, and she was hoping it would spread among the others. After arriving back in the large room where everyone was resting, Judy had David turn on the large propane burner to heat the stew. Sara poured the cans of stew into a big pot, and announced "dinner would be ready soon." This would surely perk everyone up with a big smile.

Catherine came up, "Mother are we going to have some crackers with our stew?"

"Yes, I'm glad you ask," Judy said. "Would you be nice enough to go find some on food rack C, in the back?"

"I'm scared to go back there by myself." Catherine said.

"Sara, would you go back to the food racks where we just came from with Catherine, and get some crackers from rack C, please?"

With a big smile, Sara said, "I am so glad you are letting me help you this way, because it helps keep my mind off the problems that we are having, Catherine and I will be right back." In about five minutes, Catherine handed Judy two tubes of crackers, that she was ask to go get.

"From now on get only one tube, because we will have to conserve with our limited food supply, ok Catherine." Catherine nodded "ok." After getting a nod from Catherine, Judy called out, "Everyone look this way, dinner is ready, over on the big table with the oil lamps."

Dr. Vickers and his wife waiting for everyone else to be seated, walked over, and sat down with their bowl and spoon in hand.

"If it's okay I would like to say the blessing before we start eating?" David asks.

James says, "I thank that is a good idea" and bowed his head. After the blessing, everyone was enjoying the hot stew, alongside the constant warm yellow light of the oil lamps.

During the meal, David stood up, looking at his wife sitting next to him and said to everyone "My wife and I are very grateful that James and his wife Judy picked us up on the freeway earlier. It would have been extremely doubtful if either of us would have survived."

"We are all here to help each other the best way we can, and it will take all of us working together, to accomplish this." James commented.

Chapter Three

James and David had just sat down, when the entire cave shuddered violently, some big rocks tumbled down from the ceiling, and the two oil lamps on the table turned over. No one screamed or even said a word, just stunned with the dust all around them. Dr. Vickers and Sara picked up the oil lamps, amazed, that they were still burning and sat them back on the table.

"I don't know where that missile touched down, but the navigation gyros must have not been accurate because there is nothing of importance over here in this westerly section of the state," James said.

When everyone was seated, at the large wooden table with just the oil lamps giving off their warm light, at just that moment there was a loud pounding on the steel door. Everyone stayed seated; they were so startled except James, who was getting up and asked, "Judy get my suit for protection." James walked over to the electric gauge for the 12-volt deep cycle battery pack, and saw it was now reading eleven volts. James then said, "Hey, everyone the solar panels did their job by charging the batteries and washing them off worked. It's nine thirty at night now and we will be using the TV monitor outside the steel door with the light."

"The pounding has started again, but this time much weaker, we are going to have to let them in now; I just know they are hurt!" commented Sara.

"Not yet, not until everyone gets their suits on." James said, now suited again in his protective suit and head protection and goggles. Walking over to a table in the corner, James uncovered the TV monitor and other electronics equipment, where he turned two switches on. The TV monitor came on, with the bright flood light clearly showing the steel door from the outside. "That is Dr. Rogers, the dentist I spoke to about three weeks ago, and the lady, on the ground, I do not recognize; let's open the door quickly,"

James shouted. As the door swung open slowly, James could see some of the destruction from the burning fires all around. Many of the trees were on the ground, broken like cord wood, grass still smoldering, in just one big mess. James and Dr. Rogers pulled the young woman inside and the others started closing the door.

"Your friend seems to be hurt very bad let's put her on a stretcher," Dr. Vickers instructed.

"No," James stated, "she will have to be decontaminated first, for her safety and the safety of the others here."

"Start the propane furnace for the hot water quickly," Judy said, "we have a lot of work to do!"

"While we wait for the water to get hot, I will explain to Dr. Rogers what decontamination process has to be done. You have to throw away all of your clothes you have on including your pager and wallet in that hole with the yellow lid on it. Then wash every inch of your body to do away with any radioactive material that might be on your skin. Your woman friend will need the same; even her burns need washing and her hair. If you cannot clean her yourself maybe, one of us could help. Maybe Dr. Vickers should attend her since you are so weak. Dr. Vickers do you think you and your wife could wash this young woman up, please?"

"Yes, Martha let's get busy, you wash her hair and I will attend to these burns. What is her name?" Dr. Vickers questioned and noticed the severity of the burns on her face, arms, and back.

"James my girl friend's name is Betty Goodbye and she is thirty one years old." Dr. Rogers said. Miss Goodbye was experiencing severe pain and that was evident in her face.

Dr. Rogers and his girl friend had just finished their shower and had tested negative for any radiation.

"Dr. Vickers, and David," James requested, "please escort them over to the medical / recovery room." The room is a shell, built of wood boards, covered with very heavy plastic all over including top and sides with a wooden floor. Dr. Rogers walked slowly while Dr. Vickers and David carried Betty through the opening of the door. Dr. Rogers, not feeling well, when he was nearing the medical room, noticed it had a double passageway of heavy plastic, which closed behind them each time they passed through. Dr. Rogers was familiar to air lock passageways, but never in a primitive shelter like this. When they were both inside and their eyes had adjusted to all the LED white lights, Dr. Rogers noticed everything was very well equipped. David helped Betty to pull up to the head of the bed to get comfortable. After seeing, Betty was on the stretcher safely, Dr. Rogers got on the other stretcher. James walked in now wearing a surgical smock and head wrap with a facemask to help keep from contaminating Betty or Dr. Rogers at this critical stage and sat down at the foot of the bed, between both of them.

"Dr. Vickers, after you change out of your protective gear into your surgical smock I want you to pull up a chair for a minute, while I go over a few things with these two brave people."

Dr. Vickers spoke up and said, "Okay, give me a minute to change."

"First you and Dr. Rogers have been through a lot in the past few hours, we all know that. Second, Betty, your injuries are much worse, because of the burns you have received.

Dr. Vickers, great your back, would you start an IV drip of glucose and saline mixed immediately on both Betty and Dr. Rogers. Thanks to you, Dr. Vickers we have Morphine that you brought with you. You can give some to Betty for her pain. The only thing I have in the shelter for infection is tetracycline at this time and we will make it work. Dr. Vickers I would like your opinion on everything I am covering. Have I left anything out?" James asked Dr. Vickers.

"No," and Dr. Vickers got up and started rolling two IV stands over to the bed. "Both of you are very lucky that you came to this shelter. James has covered everything I can think of," Dr. Vickers said, "except the burns on Betty's face and arms and whether or not you have taken morphine before. Does it make you throw up Betty, if so I will look for something else for pain?"

"Those burns are going to be just fine," James, stated, "there will be some scaring, I hope very little. Betty, I will be using unprocessed honey on your burns. The same as was used back in Moses time, with excellent success and for hundreds and hundreds of years after that. The reason everyone quit using honey in my opinion is there is more profit in drugs than in honey." Then James turned and said, "Dr. Vickers there are a few Percocet tablets in the cabinet on the left with a "P" on the outside of the drawer they are in. Dr. Vickers got up, went to the cabinet, and opened the drawer marked P. Looking into the pulled out drawer, he saw at least two dozen tablets, reached in and got one. He then walked back over to Betty giving her the tablet with a glass of water. "Sara, glad to see you're wearing your sterile smock, and face mask. Would you get some type of chicken soup with crackers please for two, thank you?" Sara nods ok to James as he continues to talk to the newcomers. "I think its past time for both of you to have something to eat and Betty, you need something on your stomach, with that pill. Get me a pot of hot water at 90 degrees Dr. Vickers please," James asks. With his head back, eyes closed and a tired face, James looked exhausted with everything he had done that day.

In around ten minutes, Sara brought in the soup, saying, "If this is not enough I'll make you two some more." Dr. Vickers brought in the pot of hot water and James put two jars of honey into the water. "This honey will spread much better when it is just under body temperature." James indicated to Dr. Vickers to be seated so they could get started.

"Betty, do you have any questions before we get started, because this is not going to take long at all?"

"Yes, I do," with tears 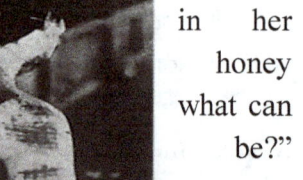 in her eyes now. "How is the honey going to heal my burns and what can I expect the healing time to be?" Betty questioned.

"Betty why don't you hold your boyfriends hand while I explain how this is going to take place. We haven't given him much attention and he is very concerned also." Betty reached over, took Dr. Rogers hand, and smiled the best she could.

"Now," James said, "with burns, infection is your biggest enemy. That is why only a very few will be coming into this room and those that do, will be dressed like Dr. Vickers and myself. Now to answer your question Betty, I believe your burns will be much, much better in three weeks and significantly better in four weeks. That is for your burns only. The radiation is another matter. I will not know until a week or two weeks, depending on the amount of radiation sickness you experience. Let's get back to your burns now," James said. "This honey I will be using contains proteins and enzymes that are antibacterial and antiviral releasing hydrogen peroxide on contact, killing germs and providing oxygen to speed up your burn healing. Even in the burn centers in hospitals, patients are routinely bathed in oxygen to enhance healing and keep down infection. Are you in the pain that you were an hour ago, Betty?"

"Not near as much as I was, but I still am very nervous," Betty answered.

"Ok, let's get started so you two can get some sleep," James stated, as he was pouring the honey into a small sterile flat container. "Would you hold Betty's arm still so we want get honey all over her, Dr. Vickers?" As Betty's arm was being held steady, James started the warm honey flowing on Betty's arms until all the burn area was completely covered. "Are you comfortable, Betty, in the position you are laying now, because I'm going to cover your face and neck next?"

"Yes, I am very comfortable thank you and the pain is almost all gone away."

"James, now that we are thru dressing Betty's arm I am going to take the temperature of Dr. Rogers. When you are through with dressing her face and neck and her back, please start a chart for both of them tonight?" Dr. Vickers asks.

"Dr. Vickers, I would like you to cut back on Betty's Morphine drip a little for the night so she will not get nauseated and throw up," James commented. When James turned around, he saw Dr. Vickers putting a thermometer in Betty's and Dr. Rogers mouth. James started pulling sheets and blankets over both Betty and her boyfriend Dr. Rogers.

James said, "Judy will be staying with you all night and if you needed anything just tell her and she would take care of it." James excused himself and said he was going to take radiation readings outside with the remote probe, to be transmitted to headquarters.

As James left the medical recovery room, he noticed the cool fifty-four degree air in the large master room where everyone was sleeping. It was so quiet, cool, and empty and he felt so alone.

James walked over to the electronics on the wooden table and uncovered the single side band transceiver that he had put there a few years earlier and a radiological monitor that measures the radiation with the help of an outside probe. James knew he was already one hour late on reporting the radiation level outside the shelter to Mission Control in Atlanta, Georgia by Morse code. James turned on the radiological survey meter and the transceiver to warm up so the frequency could stabilize and there would not be a frequency drift.

While everyone was sleeping, James looked at the survey meter, which was now reading just under two hundred roentgens. That last explosion, that burned Betty so bad, was really closer than I expected James thought. With the radiation being so high, he knew that anyone outside would not last very long.

James pulled his chair up to the table to tune in the correct frequency of Mission Control. James had been a radio operator on a Navy ship when he was younger, so this was not new to him, and that was why he was selected as Shelter Manager by the government. James put his hand on the key, to start sending the Morse code and thought, being all alone with everybody sound asleep around him, and those in need of medical attention, trying to heal, that he had not done such a bad job, for the first day. Just then, James heard the Morse code being sent threw his earphones that he was sending out to Mission Control, telling the number of people in the shelter and how many were injured, the radiation level outside and the amount of water and provisions available. He knew Mission Control in Atlanta had been waiting on this information. It is no telling what they thought had happened with Number Five Shelter, since they had not heard anything until now.

James then went back into the medical room to check on Betty and Dr. Rogers, and ask Judy, his wife "how everyone was doing?"

"We are all doing just fine; you need to get some sleep." Judy commented.

"You are right dear, I do need to lie down, and I am very tired." James went and retired for the evening on a cot in the main room.

Chapter Four

James opened his eyes in the cool darkness of the caves vast emptiness and smelled coffee swirling around him. Looking over his shoulder, James saw just about everyone sitting around one oil lamp drinking coffee and talking among themselves very quietly. He sat up feeling the dampness on his face and a chill over his body. Putting on his shoes and walking over to wash off his face, James looked over to the recovery room and wondered how things went while he was sleeping. James walked over to the group by the oil lamp and said 'good morning' to everyone with a big smile. Sara handed him a cup of coffee with one sugar and kissed him on the cheek. Looking surprised, James smiled, "if that is the case, I think I will have two cups!" With two cups in his hands, James went into the recovery room, putting on his mask to protect those inside. He saw his wife Judy sitting in a chair looking up at him with her mask still covering her face. He could tell by her eyes and her flyaway hair that she was very tired and needed sleep and rest.

"My dear, go outside and find a cot with two blankets to get some rest, handing her the cup of coffee." James then looked over at Dr. Rogers and Betty, still sleeping soundly. He was so gratified they were resting comfortably. James noticed Betty's forehead being very damp and reached for the thermometer. A high fever is one unfortunate side effect of radiation retention. Betty opened her eyes as James put the thermometer in her mouth, but did not move. Still holding the thermometer James looked over at Dr. Rogers, who was just waking up and looking over at them, with a smile.

"Did you sleep well?" James asked.

Dr. Rogers nodded "yes, and I am hungry."

"That's a good sign, I will bring you a bowl of oatmeal," smiling as James left. Walking back to the food stores with his flashlight, James was thinking what today would be like.

It was cold and pitch dark, while walking to the food stores sections, in the back of the cave. The small flashlights beam did not seem to go any distance at all, as James strained to see. Then James heard a noise directly ahead. While straining to see, with the small flashlight James tripped over a small box that had been pulled from the shelf. Pulling himself up off the dusty ground, shining the flashlight on the busted open box, that was marked aspirin. James quickly thought to himself, I surly hope no one is taking the medical supplies or food without asking! Just then, a small figure walked into view.

"Bill, what in the world are you doing here?" James asked. James son did not say anything at first, then started crying, looking at his dad holding the aspirin.

"You were so busy with Dr. Rogers and Miss Goodbye in that medical room that I didn't want to tell you Catherine is real sick and has a headache."

"When did you find out about Catherine not feeling well, Bill?"

"This morning, Dad, after we got up and before we started talking."

Chapter Five

"Bill, we need to quickly find your sister! Shine your flashlight in front of you like I am doing, and let's go back to the beds."

Bill was walking directly behind his dad, in big strides, out of the food storage room, not wanting the darkness to surround him too much. One more corner to turn and they would be back with everyone else in the big room, when all of a sudden Bill was knocked down to the dirt floor by a thunderous explosion, coming from the large room where everyone was gathered. James turned and asks, "Bill, are you ok," when a wall of dust hit both of them. This was all James needed now when his daughter needed him desperately and another emergency was right in front of him! James pulled Bill up from the dirt floor and started moving toward the medical room. Once inside he handed his son a mask and put one on himself, asking, and "Is everyone ok?"

Dr. Rogers asks, "Is everything ok?"

"I do not know what has happened yet, but am in the process of finding out, Bill stay inside the medical shelter shielded from the dust." With that, he grabbed ten more mask to hand out and went outside. Once outside and his eyes adjusting to the darkness, James saw one large bolder sitting in the middle of the room which broke away from the ceiling. The large bolder was about twenty feet in diameter and sitting on two of the last cots that was put in the large room for sleeping and resting. *It was just one big mess, James thought!* James then started walking around checking on everyone's condition, handing out the mask and asking where his daughter, Catherine was. It was hard to see over six feet in front of him, so James went to the cot where Catherine usually sleeps. There he found his little daughter bundled up under a blanket, not moving.

James asks, "Catherine, how are you feeling?" as he knelt down by her cot. Catherine turned over and looked up at her dad, but was not smiling. James put his hand on her forehead, and immediately could tell she was burning up with a fever. James told Catherine, "stay right here and I will be right back." Then James went looking for Dr. Vickers, the General Physician he had persuaded to join the shelter. Dr. Vickers was sitting on his cot holding his wife, Martha, when James found him.

"Martha, would you mind if I borrow your husband for a few minutes, my daughter Catherine is very sick?" As soon as I finished asking, Dr. Vickers got up and started walking with me.

"I found her with a fever and do not know what is causing it, Dr. Vickers." We both walked up to the cot where Catherine was sitting and Dr. Vickers bent down to take her temperature.

"She doesn't feel good because she has a temp of one hundred and three. Give me your flashlight." Dr. Vickers said to James. Dr. Vickers turned the light on Catherine, with his eyes wide open in disbelief, there was a look in his face that James had never seen before.

"Where did you get this coat that you are wearing Catherine?" James looked at Dr. Vickers strangely, as he asks this question. Dr. Vickers turned to James and said, "This is the same coat I was wearing when I came in from the outside, *it is highly contaminated.*"

"I told you to throw all your clothes down the hole in the ground when you first came in the shelter and decontaminate after that, James screamed!" James trying to think what to do next was beside himself with fear for his daughter. Dr. Vickers grabs a long stick.

"Catherine take off that coat as fast as you can and place it on the tip of this stick." Dr. Vickers says. Catherine then hung the coat on a stick that Dr. Vickers was holding out in front of him. Once the coat was on the stick Dr. Vickers ran around the rock wall and threw the coat down the hole and thought, *that is where it should have gone the first time, I walked in the door.*

James ran over and turned on the propane-heating unit, so Catherine could get under a warm shower. The contaminated dust will have to be washed off his daughter right away to keep any other damage from occurring. James ran over to the cot where his wife, Judy was sleeping, and woke her up to explain the bad news.

"I need you to take all her clothes off and let her take a good warm shower to get the contamination off, right away."

"Do you think she will be all right darling?" Judy ask her husband.

"Looking down at the ground, with a long face, James said, "The outlook is very bad. The coat was left on a long time, and because of that and the fact that she is a small little girl, will be against her." With that, Judy started moving toward her daughter's cot and James going back into the medical room.

"Dr. Rogers, I am sorry for not getting back sooner with the oatmeal for you and Miss Goodbye. I had a few things go bad this morning but I do have your oatmeal now piping hot."

"Is everything ok and is there anything I can do? I feel better after resting," said Dr. Rogers.

"Just get some more rest and make sure Miss Goodbye eats her oatmeal. She needs it to build her strength up. I will check on you two in a little bit." After this statement, James left to check on the others.

After checking on everyone else, James knew he had to contact Mission Control this morning, so he went to his desk and uncovered his equipment and turned it on to warm up. Sitting down to select the correct frequency on the transmitter, James started to transmit. The number of injured, the condition of food and water supplies and the important level of radiation outside.

Contamination level was what Mission Control was waiting for. The radiation level will be necessary for Mission Control to compare with other locations in the state so they can direct troop movement through that area.

Chapter Six

The radiation had dropped significantly outside, in James opinion, so that was a step in the right direction. James had noticed the voltage had dropped a little on the deep cycle Twelve-volt batteries that run the radio equipment. And something has to be done about this low voltage. This meant another trip outside to the solar cells on top of the hill, and James was not looking forward to going outside because of the radiation, but also seeing the carnage done by the missiles.

James then walked into the medical room to check on his daughter. His wife, Judy was sitting by her bed watching Catherine and taking her temperature. She then looked at James and shook her head, with her eyes closed. This was a terrible time for both James and Judy, James thought to himself.

"Judy, I hate to tell you this. Nevertheless, I have to go back outside to clean the solar panels."

Judy nodded her approval saying, "I need to take care of our daughter." James then walked over to the decontamination side of the shelter to put on his suit to protect him from the remaining contamination outside. David McDaniel knew there was a certain amount of danger involved in cleaning those solar panels on the hill and did not want to do this job himself.

After putting on his protection suit and getting his head gear on, James picked up the bucket of water and brush to wash the solar panels, and asked, "David, please help open the door?"

Everyone stood back while the huge door started grinding open. "Open the door just enough for me to squeeze through," James said, and that is when the door stopped moving. James then stuck his head through the opening to look out. It was daylight with smoke filling the air. There were twisted limbs everywhere and a small amount of burnt ash on the ground. James knew that this ash was where the contamination would be, and without stirring it up to much, James started to make his way up the hill to the solar panels. As he was getting close to those large impressive panels, James looked at the skies to the east, where a huge amount of smoke was still filling the sky. He then knew the decision to choose a shelter fifty-five miles west of Atlanta was so important to him and everyone inside.

Then James turned and looked at the condition of the solar panels, covered with leaves and a lot of fall out ash and dust, which he knew had to be cleaned off very gingerly, in order not to create a lot of radioactive dust. Using the water and brush, which he had brought with him, James worked very slowly in order not to stir up the dust too much. James then started back down to the shelter entrance, when he saw a truckload of men heading his way.

James then started to run toward the shelter door as fast as he could as all eight men started moving toward him. Just getting inside before one man grabbed the door screaming profanities at him. "Dr. Rogers and David I need you help immediately."

"Dr. Rogers and David, without your help pushing the huge door closed, I would not have been able to bolt the door without those men getting in and causing no telling how much trouble. Thanks." James breathless told Dr. Rogers, and David, and they nodded they were glad to be of help. Immediately James goes to the electronic table knowing that he did not have very much power left in those deep cycle batteries. Looking over at the voltmeter, he could tell they were too low to run any emergency defense system he had installed outside the shelter. Immediately James ran to the side of the propane tank and pushed the green start button on the large propane fueled generator. James knew this would run any electric system that was associated with this shelter, and charge the batteries quick.

Going back to the electronic table, James sat down and called aloud, "David Mc and Dr. Rogers get over here real quick, please." When they were standing over James, he turned on the two small monitors that showed the front of the shelter outside in two different positions. Both, of which showed the men now firing rifles at the front door hinges and locks. "This is why we have emergency defense!" James said.

"Sara, please get my son over to be with his mother while we try to straighten out the problem outside." With Bill gone now, James turned on the PA system outside and spoke on the microphone. "What do you want from us inside this shelter?"

"We have women and children in this shelter that are sick and hurt and we cannot allow anyone threatening us with guns, do you understand?" Then there was a loud voice from the outside along with the gunshots.

"We want you to let us in now!" The man yelling was very absolute in his statement, and very threatening James thought. James pushed the microphone again and spoke.

"We have no intentions of letting you or any of your friends in as long as you show hostile threats toward any of us in this shelter." James then stated, "We will not negotiate any of these request or even discuss anything further unless you put down all of your weapons immediately." James then looked up at the two men standing above him. "Do you two think you're capable of defending this shelter?"

Both David and Dr. Rogers nodded and said at the same time, "Yes, I guess so James." Then James started explaining what has to be done in order to protect the shelter and the people inside.

"I had two defense systems installed on top of two fifty foot tall metal post. This system is called the AA 12 AUTOMATIC GUN SYSTEM {automatic assault 12 gauge shot gun} capable of firing three hundred rounds a minute with 00 buck shot. Each gun has a detachable round drum magazine, holding thirty shotgun cartridges each. The guns are protected by a three-eight inch steel box around them and I named this defense system [Big Bertha.]" James then pointed at the round red dot on the TV monitor screen.

"This is the aiming dot and moving this small joy stick will rotate the gun around to aim. In order to fire the gun push this button once and holding the button down, it will be fully automatic. Remember," James said, "you only have thirty rounds per magazine on each gun." James then turned on the PA system again and stated to the men outside they have one minute to leave and take their guns with them or they will be neutralized.

James noticed one of the men had picked up the old ten-pound sledgehammer and was starting to hit the locks. Hearing the loud banging of the sledgehammer caused concern about the effect it was having on that big steel door.

"James, how long can that hinge on the steel door hold up with all the banging from the sledgehammer?" Dr. Rogers asks. "I don't know how long the lock or hinge will hold up under that heavy pounding," James stated, watching the clock. "We're going to give them one full minute." You could see the stress in everyone's face now, with the seconds clicking by. "James come quick," Judy screams out, "our daughter is much worse, with a higher fever!"

"Dr. Rogers come with me please." At this point James suddenly stops, turns to David, "Can you handle the situation outside?" David nodded "yes." Then they proceeded to the medical room.

Dr. Rogers quickly checked Catherine's temperature and found it to be one hundred and four degrees. He then put a cool wet towel over her face, sat her up and gave her a strong Tylenol tablet with water.

"Judy keep the cold towel over Catherine's forehead and face for one hour and if the temperature does not come down we will put her in a cool sitz bath to bring the temperature down. Judy increase Catherine's antibiotics for three days then go back to normal." James and Dr. Rogers then walked back to the electronics table, where David was still sitting quietly, not moving, looking at the TV monitor. There on the TV monitor were seven bodies lying on the ground outside. James looking at the monitor said he only counted seven, where was the eighth body. David looked up with tears in his eyes, "I am sorry, he ran back to the car and left." James knew that might be a problem in the future.

"We will have to have a group to go outside to bury the bodies very soon. I cannot go because of the exposure time I received when I went to clean the solar panels outside. The holes have all ready been dug, before we entered the shelter," James commented.

"How many holes did you dig? How did you know you would need them?" David asks.

"I was told by Mission Control to be prepared. We may have to put two or three to a grave because I only dug a few."

Chapter Seven

James sat down at the transmitter and turned it on along with the receiver to warm them up. He then turns around and says, "David, I have to notify Mission Control of the incident."

James then started transmitting Morse code to control for about five minutes about the men, how many killed, and who escaped. Also, the ones that are sick in the shelter and their condition, the existing food supply, along with the all-important radiation level outside. In about twenty minutes, Mission Control starting transmitting back with information about sending a squad of fully armed troops plus extra supplies for the shelter, which will arrive in about twelve hours. After James copied the message down and read it aloud, everyone was very surprised. James walked into the medical room to check on his daughter and wife, both of whom were doing better than expected, considering the circumstances.

"Hey, James is it okay to turn off the generator?" David hollered.

James then remembered it was still running and said, "OK. Let's all eat and clean up before the troops get here, also everyone break out some more folding beds and put them along the rock wall over there, out of the way. This shelter could turn out to be a real lively place, real soon with these troops arriving." James then went to the medical room to check on everyone including his daughter and wife who has been at Catherine's side all the time she was recovering from radiation poisoning. Catherine looked very nice and comfortable sitting up eating a bowl of soup with crackers. This type of food is very important for the patients with radiation sickness, in order for them not to get dehydrated due to the upset stomach or diarrhea that it turns into. Sara was cleaning up all around the general area; she seemed to be doing usually well.

"James," Dr. Rogers said, walking into the medical shelter. "I wanted to let you know that I checked your daughter over real well yesterday, and found no abscesses in her mouth." James was very pleased in hearing this news because he knew that abscesses on the teeth was an indication to the amount of radiation someone receives.

David sticks his head in the door of the medical room. "James I need to speak to you for a minute."

Looking concerned, James comes to the door. "What is the matter?"

"I thank I found **GOLD**," David commented quietly in James ear.

"David, what are you talking about? Where do you think you found gold?" Looking surprised says James.

"I was looking around way in the back of the shelter and found a hole in the wall that led to a cave shaft and look what I found." David said. Bringing out a large piece of quartz rock, and placing it in James hand, David commented, "This is the best thing that has happened to me in months." James, having had some experience in gold himself, sat down on a large bolder and turned on his light he always carries with him to examine the rock. To his surprise, the quartz rock did have an unusually large streak of gold running through it.

"If you can find the location again and if there was a substantial vein in the shaft you and your wife will be a very rich couple." James looked at David and smiled.

David looked at James, with a very serious face; "Any gold I find in this cave will be shared with you and Judy, your wife, for picking my wife and I up off the street after the bomb fell a few months back."

"Actually all eleven of us in the cave are trying to survive, should share equally in the gold, because we are all one big family, trying to help each other in bad times."

David's big smile indicated he liked James idea and gave the rock back to James to show the others.

"Before the troops get here with the supplies, let's look where you found this gold," James said, starting to move in that direction.

Stopping to pick up a flashlight from his wife, "Sara, I will be back shortly, listen out for the troops that will be showing up soon." David turns to catch up with James to show him the location.

Moving to the rear of the cave David and James were both walking slowly in order not to trip or fall over sharp rocks jutting out from the walls of the cold wet cave.

"I never knew it could be so dark until I started exploring this tunnel of the cave," David commented to James.

"That's why you never want your lights to go out, in here, because you probably will never get back to safety. Just how far do we have to go to get to the location of the gold?" James asked.

"About five minutes I hope," David replied, breathing hard, as he moved swiftly along the rugged floor of the cave.

James stopped. "David what, in the world, were you doing this far back in the cave anyway? I hope you know it is very dangerous back here at any time especially by yourself."

In about ten minutes of continued walking, David grabbed James arm and had him stop to look around. "You know I should have marked the location, because everything looks the same in these dark surroundings."

James looking disgusted at David, said, "Yes you should have. We are going to have a hard time now if you can't remember and I know everything looks the same in this dark. Someone is calling us from the main room, let's go back." James motioned!

It took more than a few minutes to walk and stumble back to the large area that everyone was gathered. Both David and James were sweating and chilled at the same time from the cold damp air in the cave and were looking for some way to clean up.

"Where in the world have you been all this time?" Both men were surprised, when they heard Sara speak up. David, looked so tired when he looked up at her and said, "Not to be mad at him, because he was just trying to locate the spot where he had found the gold deposit."

"We'll have to worry about that later," Sara stated. "The troops will be here any time now and we have everything ready."

"Good," David said and started to wash his face, to remove some of the dirt from the cave trip.

"Glad to see you up and about Betty, but don't overdo. You're still healing." David cautioned Betty.

"Don't worry about me overdoing Sara has been keeping a tight rope on my activity." Betty responded.

"Good for you Sara." Sara nods and motions for Betty to go get some rest, which she does. Betty and Sara both had been setting up the cots, for the troops that were scheduled to arrive soon with new supplies for the entire group and hopefully some medical supplies also. James came over and turned on the monitor and the outdoor camera system to look around. James then pointed a finger at the monitor saying the troops were arriving. Eight had jumped out of the truck and were starting to unload the supplies.

"Turn on the LED lights now in the cave because their eyes will have to adjust to the dark and turn on the propane to heat the water so we can decontaminate them when they come in." As soon as James said that, there was a loud banging on the steel door. James picked up the microphone and started talking to the troops on the outside.

"You are being watched by closed circuit video. We will open the door for all of you in just one second but you must understand what to do when you come inside. Everyone will enter single file, carrying the supplies your bringing in and the extra clothes, then stand behind the rock wall to be decontaminated." The door started to open slowly.

James instructed, "Only two feet, and watch for those that cannot follow directions!" The first soldier entered the shelter caring his pack and a large box of supplies followed by the next. Each, soldier was directed where to stand, and what to do, by James and David.

James directed all the women to sit in the back, away from the men coming in to keep from becoming exposed to radiation and give the soldiers some privacy when they are taking a shower to decontaminate.

"Okay men, I need you to use the soap all over; including your hair, to be one hundred percent clear of radiation and empty your pockets then dump your uniforms in the big hole against the wall with the yellow lid on top. This is very important for your health as well as ours." Dr. Vickers instructed.

"Dr. Vickers, tell the troops they will be served soup for supper tonight with crackers in about an hour."

After the troops finished their soup, an officer asks, "Which one of you is James Cummings, the shelter manager? I need to talk to you about the reason we are at the shelter." The officer stood, "I am the Officer in Charge, Greg Potters, with the Marines."

James shook his hand and told how much he appreciated him and his troops being there and especially with the supplies, they brought with them. At that time, Officer Potters, called over Medical Officer Andy Wallace, who had been assigned to the platoon as the Medic in case there was no qualified doctor in the shelter.

"Officer Potter and Officer Wallace, I have two doctors that I found two years earlier that have been working with me and this group, but I would appreciate Officer Wallace to look at the three patients that are in the sick room as soon as possible."

Officer Potters then spoke up, "I need to sit down and talk to the entire group."

"Only after the sick are examined will that be possible." James said. With that said Dr. Vickers, Dr. Rogers, and Officer Wallace made their way to the medical room. James daughter Catherine, was sitting up besides her mother Judy, recovering from the exposure to radiation, along with Betty Goodbye, who was healing from her burns.

James turned to Officer Wallace, "I would like you to meet my daughter Catherine, whom I think is very brave and I am very proud of her, considering everything she has been through. She didn't realize that the coat she was wearing at the time was contaminated until it was too late."

"Catherine has not been running a fever in the last few days and does not have an upset stomach," Dr Vickers stated. "Nor does Catherine have any abscesses in the mouth or nausea at this time."

"Betty is also in the medical room, recovering from burns that she received in the first explosion and seems to be doing very well," James commented.

"We could use any type of medical supplies that you may have brought with you, Officer Wallace."

Chapter Eight

"Please would each of you sit at the big table here outside the medical room?" Officer Potter requested, when James and Officer Wallace stepped out of medical room, after checking on Catherine and Betty Goodbye.

"I want to inform everyone the troops are going to be at the shelter for about a week, to protect everyone against any more aggravation. The government has determined this particular shelter is very important to take a chance of anything else happening. Hope you do not mind.

Each of you knows that the shelter is located very close to the major freeway traveling East and West and is the main highway the government will send the troops on, too relocate them and therefore the radiation has to be monitored at all times."

"If we are to eat, we need to get busy. Everyone needs to go back to his or her duties so the next meal can be prepared on time and the battery system can be checked out." James announced.

"Officer Potter, I just noticed that the volt meters the deep cycle batteries are that low and the solar panels on top of the mountain probably have trash on them. Would it be possible if one of your men could go up and clean the leaves off the solar panels?"

"Of course, James." Officer Potter responded.

"Let me check the radiation level outside first, to insure his safety. I am, fairly sure, the level is down substantially by this time. I want to monitor the young marine by video camera to make sure he does not get hurt and if he does we will be aware of the incident." James said.

Officer Potter assigned a young marine to do the cleaning and come right back down.

The big door was now opening and the young marine quickly slipped outside to climb the hill. After finishing he came right back in, showered and hung up his suit he wore outside for later use.

"David let your wife Sara and Judy know I am going back into the cave to try to find the gold deposit that you located, yesterday."

"Okay, but I am going also," David said. David proceeded to tell both wives and they nodded okay. He picked one big flashlight and extra batteries while James did the same. With gloves in their back pocket, both of them headed back into the dark cave. The cave was the same, cold damp place, as both of them continued to navigate the uneven floor of the cave.

David turned to James and said, "We are looking for that large vein of quartz that is in the wall, and it's on the right side. That's where the gold will be."

About five minutes later, "David, I need to sit down a few minutes to rest." While James was resting, David sat on a large rock that had dislodged and fallen down off the sidewall of the cave. David turned the flashlight up to the wall to see from where it fell. That is when David started jumping up and down and hollering, "James, this is the place, look up above you!" James looked at David like he had gone crazy and turned around, looking up with his flashlight shining on the black rock wall above both of them. James motioned for David to stop hollering.

Sure enough, there was the big quartz rock jutting outward, jagged, and very sharp from where David had taken a big piece of quartz from its side.

"This is a major gold find and we need to talk quietly," James stated, looking at David. "I am very pleased for all of us, because we will need the money in order to get started again, when we get out of here. There will be absolutely nothing left for us to go back to after this is over. We did not bring enough tools to work on this size quartz rock, in the wall. Let's start back so we can get some supper, before its gets too late," James commented.

"Let's mark this area with your handkerchief, so we can make sure we'll have no trouble finding it later," David stated, looking at James. David commented, "At least we found the spot we were looking for, when we started out."

"Don't you think we can leave that large quartz rock you are holding in your hand here, instead of caring it all the way back to the main room? David, would you mind keeping this gold find, just between you and I, and not mention it to the troops at all. I think it would be better for all of us in the end. When the troops leave in about a week, we will sit down and discuss everything with the rest of the folks in the shelter." James quietly said.

"Let's get started back so we can get some supper, all this walking has gotten me hungry," James stated.

With flashlights in hand James and David started the long journey back through the dark cold, narrow cave tunnel toward the main room, where both their wives were waiting, along with the Marines, and the rest of the shelter personnel.

When they arrived, everyone was sitting down at a big table eating some food that the troops, brought when they came to the shelter. We walked over and took a closer look. Because the kerosene lanterns did not give off much light, it was hard to tell what they were eating. Looked like some type of meat that came out of an open can that was sitting on the table.

My wife and Sara fixed what we found to be some type of ham, some green beans, along with crackers on the side and of course water to drink. David and I washed our hands and sat down besides our wives. Everyone was talking about different things.

When Officer Potter spoke up and ask me, "What was on the rest of today's schedule?"

"When I finish my supper, the outside radiations readings have to be taken and transmitted to Washington and the voltage on the twelve volt deep cycle batteries has to be checked, after the solar panels were cleaned." James committed.

With that said, Officer Potter committed, "I need to schedule a private meeting with you later in the day." James nodded his approval.

"Medical Officer Andy Wallace, would you be kind enough to check on those who are sick in the medical room?" James stated as he stood up when the rest of the group at the table were through with supper.

Medical Officer Wallace said, "James, I on my way to the medical room at this time and will confer back with you if anyone is in a serious condition."

"Officer Potter, I want you to watch the radiation results from the probe outside since you have never seen this device before."

"David, please connect the detector to the plug on the side wall of the cave, in order for us read the radiation outside." James knew he could trust David to hook up the connectors correctly. James sat down at his transmitter and receiver and flipped the switch on, which allowed his electronic equipment to warm up and stabilize. After he completed his transmissions to Washington of the radiation level, and the condition of his sick, still in the medical room, he sat back and waited for acknowledgment that the transmission was received. Washington is always awaiting this transmission to make notes on their maps of radiation throughout the United States, so they can have an overview of the conditions in order to be able to route their convoys safely through the country.

Officer Potter questioned, "What are the readings on the meter?"

James explains, "Those amounts are roentgens, which is the strength of the radiation outside. At the present time it is reading at approximately two roentgens." This was more than James expected, because of the time that elapsed since the initial explosion took place and now. James had thought that the radiation level would be one roentgen or below but evidently the rain had brought down additional radiation in the area of the shelter.

"Officer Potter, when you and your officers and the other Marines you have with you start back to the location you left initially, you are going to have to make a very quick trip, because this type of radiation level is more than you need to be subjected to. Decontaminate, when you get back to your location, as soon as possible or you will be in serious trouble later. After I receive conformation that the transmission of information back to Washington concerning the radiation is received we will sit down and have that discussion that you mentioned to me earlier. We got my conformation from Washington." James stated.

James stood up and motioned to Officer Potter to grab a chair and flashlight and to follow him back in the cave to the supply room where they could have complete privacy for the discussion. With flashlights in one hand and the chair in the other both James and Officer Potter made their way slowly through the dark cave until they arrived at the supply room where they sat down and lit a kerosene lantern where James awaited to find out what Officer Potter had to say.

"James my men and I will be leaving in three days as we were instructed, and we are going to leave with your group some defensive equipment in order for you and the people you have with you to defend yourselves when we are not around. Even though, those automatic guns outside on those fifty-foot poles are very efficient, the government still thinks that your group needs additional guns and supplies to protect yourselves properly. Included in the supplies are some explosive devices, which are called plastique and detonators to go with them. James these explosives are harmless unless the detonators are hooked to them and will require a 12 volt battery to explode the detonators."

James Immediately indicated, "We definitely will be glad to accept anything that the government has to offer. We do not know how long the shelter will be closed up, and it will depend on the radiation level outside."

Officer Potter said, "I will have to instruct you and your men on the proper way of using the equipment before we leave."

"Is it possible to break those plastique bars in half instead of exploding the entire bar?" James asked Officer Potter.

Officer Potter indicated, "Yes, it could be done, if they wanted to, as long as the detonator was pushed into the bar when fired."

When James got back to the main room where everyone was sitting around, James found David, Dr. Vickers, and Dr. Rogers and told them, "Officer Potter has explosives for us for protection. We need to go back to the supply area for him to show us how to set this plastique." They all go back to the supply area for training.

"David, come over here a minute. We can use this plastique to get the gold out of the sidewall of the cave. Everyone is getting bored sitting around, waiting for the radiation intensity to go down outside, and you know that could take a long time, depending on if any other bombs drop outside. I pray not. We all need to get started working on the wall as soon as the troops leave in three days." James suggested.

"James, since all of our duties here are completed, we can leave any time, and will probably be leaving in the morning. After all, you have plenty of supplies and you know how to use the ammunition you have for protection."

"Betty is making very good progress with her burns, and is eager to join everyone else in this big room, which is okay for her to do. Catherine can also join in with everyone else." Medical Officer Wallace confirms.

Chapter Nine

Officer Potter was getting his troops ready, and had told all the men how to operate the rifles and the military weapons he had left with them. For safekeeping, the C-4, detonators, and dynamite were left with James.

James had Officer Potter sit down again just to be on the safe side with David and himself to explain all the equipment and especially about the explosives. Everyone was actually anticipating the troops leaving, in order to get back to normal. The extra food and guns were going to be coming in handy in the end. The next morning the departure was on scheduled.

"Officer Potter, you and your troops are loaded up at the large door as scheduled. You will have to wait until the outside of the shelter can be inspected for intruders. Now's the time to say your goodbyes to everyone, once the door is opened you want have time. The marines will have to move very quickly so we can close the door as quickly as possible." James then turned on the monitor for the camera outside for inspection. Panning the camera very slow, James was able to tell that the troop's truck was still in the same location it was when they arrived, and there was no one else outside that may cause any harm to anyone that would be going outside.

"Officer Potter, wait before you start trying to open the large door. It will have to be opened very slowly and I will be helping but not going outside, due to the exposure I have already incurred." James commented knowing he did not need the extra exposure to the radiation, even as low as it had gotten, every little bit adds up. James let David take over closing the door, went to the monitors, and watched the troops drive away on the monitor.

"As soon as you all finish closing the door, come over here. Everyone gather around so you can see the outside land, and the condition of the land. Do you remember what I told you before we first entered the shelter?" James asks.

In a resounding statement from all, "We do remember. You said that nothing would look, or be the same, from that time on."

"Wow, look at the trees," Sara said.

"Look at the sky, it is so gray." Bill said.

"You told me this could happen and I did not want to believe you. You were correct." Judy stated.

Dr. Vickers commented, "We have been here a couple of months, I would have thought that the ground would not still be smoldering, and the sky looking so gray. Look at the ash everywhere. This is nothing like I have ever seen before." After that, James turned the monitor off because he knew this was very unnerving for everyone in the shelter to watch.

While everyone was standing together, James asks, "Judy will you to go back inside the medical room and ask Betty and Dr. Rogers and Catherine if they feel good enough to join the group for a little while."

Judy gets up and asks, "Sara please help Betty, and I will help Catherine out of the medical room, so they want accidentally fall." Both women soon appeared again with everyone slowly making their way over to the large group each one covered with a blanket and a strange look on their face.

Betty Goodbye said, "This is the second time I have been out of the medical area with my burned arm and face since I arrived in the shelter and it is just as cold and scary as the first time."

"Betty, this want take long, and if you're too cold, one of us will get you another blanket.

David McDaniel, get over here and sit beside me for a short time. All of you have been wondering what we are going to do when the radiation gets low enough for us to go outside. All of us here have been very fortunate so far, having the shelter, the medical room for us to use and the food that Marines and Mission

Control provided. The radiation is still too high for us to consider venturing out, and what are we going to do when we get outside?"

"I saw all the devastation on the monitor. How are we going to get food and water, clothes and everything we need to survive outside?" Martha questions.

With a roar from everyone comes, "Yes James how do we survive outside?"

"Daddy, how much longer do we have to stay in this place?" Catherine questioned.

"Well David is going to tell all of you what we will be doing while we wait for that day to come. I will talk privately with you Catherine after David gets thru talking." James then turns to David nodding for him to take over.

David stood up and his wife Sara was stunned with surprise by her husband's involvement.

"While I was looking around the back of our shelter a few weeks ago, I found a large opening in the back wall and ventured in and found a quartz vein in the wall. I also thought I noticed some gold in one section of that quartz. When I was able to break away a large piece of the quartz and examine it closer, I was sure of it. I was able to find James later and James confirmed I was correct in my discovery. We are all going to need some type of money, when we do go outside, so what better type of currency than gold, that is known around the world. It will take all of us, working together, to separate the quartz from the gold. James will teach all of us how to pan the quartz rock concentrate, to separate the gold properly. This is what most of us will be doing in the next few months. As James stated earlier the radiation is still too high and I do not know if any of you have noticed when the monitor was on, but it is winter outside now and not a good time to venture out in the devastation. Did you not notice the snow at the top of the troop's truck when they left? This will give all of us time to do the job and James has told me there will be enough food for this period. Betty's burns are healed, almost completely according to Dr. Vickers, and Catherine is making very good progress with her radiation sickness. It will take James and me a few days to blast enough quartz rock for you to start panning."

"Sara, you and Judy can help the girls back to the medical room, where there is less dust and David and I will start working on the vein of quartz, back in the cave." James commented.

David then looked at James and said, "We had better get started, you and I have a lot of work to do." Judy worriedly looked over her shoulder and saw James and David picking up their large bags of supplies and walking into the pitch-black twisting path that led to the back of the shelter where almost none of them had been, or seen.

"Betty, be careful lying down, and I will cover you with a warmer blanket. The fresher cleaner air and warmer temperature in the safety of the medical room will make you feel better. After we get Catherine in bed, I am going to take both of your vitals." Judy committed and a few minutes later, both were warm and resting better. Judy then started taking Betty's temperature, knowing what the effects of radiation exposure could be. In addition, upset stomach, diarrhea, and possibly a sunburn effect. James had taught Judy very well, over the years.

"Betty you seem to be getting much better, even with the burns you received before you entered the shelter. The honey, that James has carefully poured over all your burns including your face has firmed up and become a very soft rubbery substance, which I think is quiet amazing. Get some rest, I going to check on Catherine, now."

Judy then went over to Catherine her daughter, who was lying on the other bed and covered her up, and asks, "How do you feel?"

After her mom finished taking her temperature, Catherine said, "I feel much better than I did a couple of days earlier." Judy knew her daughters symptoms would be the same as Betty's. Judy was finally relieved that everyone seemed to be getting better.

Chapter Ten

David looked up after walking for twenty minutes and saw the rope with the red bandana indicating the location they were supposed to be.

David looked over at James sitting his bag down and could tell he was exhausted. Both of them sat down at the same time to catch their breath.

David asked James, "How do you want to get started?"

James requested, "Get your light and let's see exactly where the vein is located to start drilling a hole. There is a good spot. Let me hold the light while you get the hand drill and hammer and start drilling." David then positioned the hand held steel drill in the back fracture in the quartz rock, and quickly came down using his big hammer to hit the drill. Every time David hit the steel drill, he would twist it a quarter of a turn.

"David this is going to be a slow process at this rate," James stated.

"I agree." Reaching into his bag, and pulling out a facemask, looking at James says, "Going to put my mask on to filter out any dust that I make with the drilling. James, you might want to do the same."

"I think I will, David that's a good idea. I found my mask in my bag and am putting it on now." James quoted.

After two hours passed, David said, "I am tired out and my arms are worn out."

James picked up the large light, and shined it on the wall where the three drilled holes were. "David, I think the explosives could be put in now." James then looked again in his bag and pulled out a substance that looked like soft clay and pinched off a small amount and began to roll it around between his hands.

"Is that plastique?" questioned David. "Yes, and I am rolling it to the diameter of the holes you drilled. I am going to cut the roll into three sections to match the three holes." James then handed one roll at a time to David, so he could insert them into each drilled location.

Once, each one was positioned David then asks, "James, can I insert the primers at this time?"

James looked at David and said, "We both need a break before we go any further. Working with detonators is a dangerous job." James held his hand out, "David, help me up so we can start back to be with the others. Let's leave the detonators close to the wall so we will not be walking with them and have an accident, because they are very sensitive. The flashlights do not seem to be as bright as before, when we came to the back of the cave." About fifteen minutes later, they heard some talking and knew they were arriving back where the group was located. Everyone quit eating, and looked up in surprise when we arrived. Some of them did not even know we had left for some reason.

As we walked in James asked, "David is that soup they are eating?"

"I do not know. Sara is that soup?" asked David.

"Yes, it is potato soup with crackers and cheese, David." Sara said.

"Would you mind fixing me some after I clean up, I am starved." David said sweetly with a smile on his face.

"Me too, Judy, will you fix me a bowl of that potato soup, crackers and cheese and a glass of water, while I start checking the radiation level outside, to determine how safe it would be to go outside in order to clean the solar panels, so we can keep the deep cell batteries charged up." As Judy comes near me, I looked up as she says, "Here's your soup and water with the crackers and cheese on the side," while sitting it down in front of me knowing I had not eaten in a long time while I looked over the radiation meter. As I looked at Judy, the frustration and anger showed, in her face, she was ready to get out of here. She looked as if cabin fever was setting in even though we were not at home but in this terrible situation having to live in this cave.

"Thanks that smells great, Judy." James quoted.

"Uh huh," Judy turns to walk away.

"Wait Judy, what's wrong?" Comes out of James mouth.

"What do you think is wrong? I am tired of this cave and so is everyone else. I wish I had stayed at home. Don't tell me I don't." and after that Judy walks away.

"Judy baby, don't you remember what you saw on the monitors?" James speaking to Judy as she walks toward the medical room.

Turning very quickly in her steps Judy yells, "YES YES YES, but that doesn't mean I don't want to be in our own home and in our own bed." Then turns and quickly disappears in the medical room.

David comes up "James, are you okay?"

"Yes, I just need to get back to the radiation levels, they look lower, come take a look David." An as, David moves toward James as asked, he sees the levels have lowered.

"James, am I seeing what I think I am seeing? The radiation level looks lower than it has been in several weeks, so this is great. Right, James?"

James spoke up, "Hey, everyone the radiation reading is low and if the level stays down we will be able to venture out for the first time since we first locked the big door." Everyone seemed to be well enough and we still have food left to eat. James quietly thought to himself, "I know we have to try to get the gold in order to have something to barter with when we get outside."

"Judy and I are going outside to clean the solar panels and will be back in a very short time." As Judy changes James checked the outside monitor to see if he could see anyone walking around outside which would be highly unlikely.

"Dr. Ralph and Tim help me open this large door." James requested.

As Judy and I stepped outside, I said, "Quickly climb up the hill, to the solar panels for cleaning. Be careful not to tear your suit you are wearing to keep the radioactive dust from contaminating you if possible. Judy, try not to stir up any more of this dust than you can get out of. This is what is referred to as fallout, which is where the radioactive material stays. It will collect on your clothes and protective suit and will not come off until we wash it off in the decontamination wash back inside. Let's wipe off the solar cells quickly and go back inside as quick as we can," James commented. While going back down the hill to the shelter, James stopped and asks, "Judy, look at how gray the sky looks. Everything is so overcast, and looks so dark for this time of day. This overcast has been caused by the dust and ash brought up from the ground by the explosion five months ago, James explained." James and Judy arrived back at the shelter very quickly and began banging on the big door to get in as soon as possible, before too much radiation was absorbed. After a few minutes, the huge door slowly opened and both of them rushed in to get washed off. Both James and Judy stood in one place, turning around in circles, while the warm water sprayed down on their head and over the suits. After the decontamination was completed, the suits were hung up for use later. James then went and sat down where then transmitter was located at to send a message to Washington at the shelter command center, where the controllers were always waiting for information to be sent in from the United States about the conditions and radiation intensity. Once, the information was transmitted, James turned around and asks everyone to gather around so he could give them an update as to the information he received back from control.

"Now that everyone is here, Betty, are you warm enough? Catherine I hope you are feeling better, got some good news." Called out James.

Both women, nodded and answered at the same time, "We are okay. Don't keep us in suspense."

"Okay, the radiation is very low now and we can venture outside for a short time. However, any extended time outside will probably make you sick. The reason is radiation does accumulate in the body over time. Therefore, we need to wait a little longer, because there is a lot of work that has to be done to get the gold out of the rock wall in the back of the cave. Another thing, we will start in the morning digging for the gold." With that final statement from James, everyone yells "Great. Finally we can go out."

"Good morning, Judy can you get Sara and Martha to gather up as many pans as all of you can find, we will need them soon." James asked.

"I will be making the first explosion in the wall in about half an hour and do not to want you to be disturbed by the noise. James, get your light and let us start to the back of the cave, to get to work. I still cannot get use to how dark it is in this cave. It is very eerie in here." David explained while arriving at the quartz site.

"It looks the same as we left it. The sight of that big solid rock wall with a long vein of quartz with a gold streak in it is very pretty. David hold the light while I put these detonators in the explosives, one at a time. These are very sensitive and have to be placed delicately into the soft plastique explosive, which has the wires hanging out." James continued until all three explosives were wired.

"David, we need to unwrap this fifty feet of wire and walk around the corner of that big bolder that will protect us." James motioned to David to get behind the bolder with him and connect the wires to the light battery. As soon as David connected the wires the entire side of the wall in the cave exploded, which startled both of them.

David did not expect the amount of dust that was produced by the explosion and he and James had to run back to the others, in order to catch their breath. Everyone was excited; by the loud explosion by the time, they arrived back.

"We are going to have to stay out here while the dust clears," David stated to the others, "probably will be in the morning before we will be able to go back and pan." Martha and Sara had helped by collecting different types of pans that they were asked to do earlier by Judy.

Later in the day, Bill, my son, asks, "Dad what are we going to use these pans for that Mom and the others collected?"

"Bill, the pans will be used to separate the gold from the quartz and black iron ore dirt from where we found it in the back of the cave earlier. We will all need to get a good night sleep and rest, because first thing after we get up and have breakfast, everyone will be going to the gold site and start separating the gold. Soon it will be time for us to try to get out of this shelter and we will need some type of money to buy things we might need. According to my training for a disaster such as we have incurred, the U.S. Dollar will not be worth anything, and the economy could be destroyed, gold will be king of the monetary system for a long time to come next to food and water. Everybody collect all your cans or anything that you can carry gold rich dirt in to pan here in the main room. Or, if you want we can pan the dirt back in the cave close to where we blew it out of the wall to save us from having to carry all that enriched dirt all the way back here. Judy is Betty going to be able to go panning with us." James questioned.

"You better believe I am going, James." Betty stated.

Chapter Eleven

"James we all talked this morning and we all want to pan at the gold site, so we want have to carry all that dirt any further than necessary."

"Okay, David get everyone that is going and tell them bring their buckets and lights so we can get started." In about five minutes, we were all walking to the back of the cave.

"The faster we get through the faster we can try to get out of this black hole." James stated.

We all arrived at the site in about fifteen minutes and started to get organized the best we could in a small environment. We all started looking over the wall and dirt that was around us.

"David look at this. I can tell right away that the quartz lying around has good size gold streaks all through it, and this is great. All of these quartz rocks need to be crushed, in order to get the gold separated during the panning procedure." After speaking to David, James immediately turns to find his son with the doctors looking over the quartz.

"Bill, get Dr. Ralph and Dr. Rogers to go back to the sleeping area and pick up some big hammers along with the big ten pound sledge hammer so we can bust up the smaller quartz rocks that is holding the gold. David and I will start picking up the smaller rocks."

While doing that I ask, "Hey, Judy get everyone to move over here near where the water is coming out of the side wall in order to be able to pan with the water."

Noticing some were having trouble panning, I got my pan and went and gathered Sara, Martha and Tim and the rest in the circle and showed them how to pan the proper way to get the most gold out of the dirt.

"Okay, the first thing to do is start with four or five handful's of dirt and add water, then shake the dirt real strong so the gold will settle to the bottom. Hold the pan with the right hand, put your left hand in the sand, and stir it up real good. Of course, if you are left handed switch your hands around. This will bring the heavy gold to the bottom where you want it to be. Watch and I will show you with this dirt I just scooped up and put in this pan. I will demonstrate with this, but we need to move over to the water so I can show you what I am talking about." James commented to everyone around him.

Sara, David's wife and all the others were looking over James shoulder while he swirled the water in circles. James shook the dirt in the pan while this was happening, letting a little lighter dirt fall out at the same time. Everyone was amazed at how easy it looked and how the loose dirt was slowly slipping away, until they saw a streak of gold in the bottom of the pan. Now everyone wanted to try to pan for gold. James tells everyone to get their pan and scoop up some dirt around the wall and start panning by the water coming from the cracks in the wall. Some started panning while the others held a light for them to see. At least they were making some head way to collect gold that they were going to need in the future. David and James continued to collect the larger pieces of quartz that contained the gold. David and James were more than impressed with what they found in the way of quantity and quality. Everyone continued to work as the hours slipped by, later and later. Panning with the weak light, was straining their eyes making everyone very tired.

"We all need to take a break and get something to eat and rest and start fresh tomorrow," David suggested.

"I think you are right," DR. Rogers said. They all agreed and started walking back to the main room to charge their flashlights and to lie down. Everyone got something to eat and a good night's sleep.

Next morning "Betty hollered the quicker we get started the quicker we will get through today," so everyone started walking back to the work sight.

They had put on the same dirty clothes they worked in yesterday, because they could not afford to wash clothes all the time. We just did not have the recourses. The cold dark walk seemed to take forever each time. This time was different though, we were getting closer to getting out of this cave finally.

Dr. Rogers said to Dr. Vickers "I am concerned about what we are going to find once we step out of the shelter though. I have very little supplies in the medical room for people that need dental work and I believe you have very little for wounds and broken bones. Forget pain meds they are almost gone. Antibiotics are low also. I believe our wives are concerned as well as the children." Work continued smoothly as the day progressed, hour after hour.

Bill called to his mom. "Mom how about some lunch?"

"Okay, good idea. Sara how about going back to the room where the food is kept and help me to get two large cans of beans and some cups to eat and drink out of. That way it will save time and everyone can keep working while we get the food hot." Sara heard Judy and nodded "OKAY." About twenty minutes later, everyone stopped work long enough to eat and drink after washing their hands in the cold water that was washing down the cave wall. Even beans tasted good when everyone was so hungry. While they were eating, David checked to see how much gold had been collected up to this point and he was astounded. David brought the big jar over to James to look at the amount of gold everyone had collected, and neither wanted to believe what they were holding.

"Hey, everybody it will not take long to have enough gold to be able to leave the cave. We need several more jars like this in order to barter outside for what we will need to survive. You know, with us being in a war as big as this one the U.S. dollar is worthless by now and the only thing that will be of any value would be food, water, medicine, and gold. We will be finding this out soon enough unfortunately when we get outside. David, I am thru eating, let's get back to crushing the gold rich quartz rock and giving it over to those who were panning."

"Okay, your right we all need to get back to work so we can get out of here." David said to James. The amount of gold that we had collected was slowly growing day by day.

Dr. Rogers asked, "How much will the gold be worth per ounce?"

James told him, "I really don't know but I am sure it has gone up a lot since the war started. If I remember, I think before the war started, it was over fourteen hundred dollars an ounce. It could be quite a bit higher by now."

Sara and Martha told David, "David our hands are freezing from the cold water flowing down the cave wall to do the panning and we are ready to go back and wash up and get warm and maybe get some food."

"I agree. Hey, everyone we have done enough panning for today. We will be measuring the amount of gold everyone has panned so far. So let's go eat and get some sleep and get warm." Everyone started the long walk back to the sleeping area, very tired and dirty.

"Well, deep subject but I know some of you might want a shower after all that dirty work we have done the last two days. We still have a lot of propane gas left in the big tanks to heat some water if anyone wanted to take a shower before they eat. Betty Goodbye, would you help me get some food from the shelves in the other room." Judy said to Betty and everyone else.

Betty said, "OK, I'll get my flashlight. Don't forget yours."

"I have my light. Thanks for going with me to get the food we will need for this evening." Judy said. Betty and I walked about one hundred feet to the room that held all the canned food on the shelves.

Betty asks me "what we were going to eat?"

Judy said, "I have no idea what anyone wants." Then Judy thought aloud, "Why not something different if that was possible."

"I agree that's a good idea. Everyone would love to have hot vegetable soup. That would be a warm up food as well as filling and healthy for everyone. We still have a lot of canned vegetables left, even after all this time we have been in the cave. Here they are, peas, butterbeans, corn, and okra mixed with potatoes and green beans. Oh, here's the tomato's. The last can of those. Glad those marines bought us the medium size cans so we can carry these easily when we leave. *Homemade potluck stew for dinner...*" Betty said to Judy with a little laughter and musically in her tone of voice.

Soon as Betty and Judy got back, Sara and Betty started opening the cans of soup mixes with our manual can opener and pouring them into a large pot with a small amount of water that Sara had started heating up.

Catherine asks, "Sara, what are you fixing?"

Sara told Catherine, "It sort of what my mother called *gumbo vegetable soup.*"

Betty chimed in and told Sara, "When I was a kid we called it *homemade potluck stew.*" Dr. Vickers and Dr. Rogers overheard the women as they walked up after taking a shower. They could not help but laugh, and ask, "Is one of those stews ready. We are all ready to eat."

Dr. Rogers continued teasing Betty, "Hey, we were told supper would ready when we finished our baths if we let all of you women go first in the shower."

"Don't start up Ben Rogers; I am too tired to horseplay with words." Betty quipped in a laughing way.

"While everyone is eating, I need to say something." With that statement, James got everyone's attention. Everyone looks up and says in unison, "What's up?"

"Each of you needs to start gathering your personal supplies to put in your emergency bags in order to leave, because time is getting close. We are going to have to pan for more gold over the next week and take inventory of the food we have left." James caused a lot of hollering of "HIP HIP HOORAY!!!" Only one more week!

Chapter Twelve

"Good morning, David, ready for a cup of coffee? I just got thru making some coffee."

"Sure I would love a cup of coffee James. Anybody else up?"

"Not yet David, we need to look with the cameras outside to check if it is safe to go outside and check the truck in the building. We need to be sure if it will crank. I hope the battery has not discharged. I am going to put the battery charger on the battery anyway just in case. I have always experienced batteries drain severely in cold weather and we had a few storms while we have been in the shelter." James said while noticing David was walking to the monitors.

David turned on the monitor, so we could look outside for any danger that might be waiting when we go out. Everyone gathered around to look outside and was astonished at what they saw when David got the monitor booted up.

There was a gray ash over everything similar as if a volcano had exploded nearby and the sun was not shining bright. It was as if there was a dark overcast limiting our field of vision outside making it very unusual.

"Dad, what is that thick gray material?" Bill questioned his dad.

James pointed out the large amount of ash that was covering everything, and explained, "This is what fallout looks like. It has gotten thicker. You will not be able to get away from this ash unfortunately no matter how soft you walk. It may be highly contaminated but I hope it is not. I am going to find out in a few minutes."

David was looking at the monitor now and commenting, "It looks so different from the time we entered the cave."

Turning around David questions James. "James do you think it will be safe for you and I to go outside after we put on our protective suits?" David turns back to the monitor as James says, "It should be okay."

David was straining his eyes now and commented, "I don't think so," and turned around and looked at James strikingly.

James asks, "David, What in the world is wrong?"

David commented, "Look."

That is when James took a closer look at the monitor showing the outside of the shelter and let out a gasp with astonishment. There sitting about thirty feet from our shelter was a man or what James and David thought was a man leaning on a big rock too weak to move very much it seemed. He had burns over fifty percent of his body and was surely suffering with pain.

David asks, "James if that man is not dead, how has he lived and how is he going to live, in the condition he is in?"

As James starts to respond to David, he realizes everyone was looking over his shoulder. "Okay, first I am extremely surprised that anyone outside would be alive at this point in time. This man with the burns he has sustained should already be dead. He probably wishes he were. I am sure he is suffering from extreme dehydration along with chronic diarrhea and am sure he is so weak he probably cannot get up. Let me tell all of you at this point that this man cannot medically be saved even by a hospital. Radiation will destroy human tissue very quickly with a very grotesques result. The amount of radiation he has received at this point is not recoverable unfortunately. We still need to go outside with the battery charger and one solar cell and a controller box today. We have to check the truck, to make sure it works."

Judy, James wife, came up to him and whispered in his ear, "Can't someone else go outside this time James?"

James told his wife very quietly, "This trip going outside will be a very important one and probably be very uncomfortable and unnerving."

"Are you ready?" David asks as he tapped James, on the shoulder.

James nodded ok and ask, "Judy can you and Sara help David and me with our protective suits, gloves and boots. Our whole body will have to be covered to protect us from all the ash that will be stirred up when we walk outside." James stepped into his suit first and zipped it up, then put on the rubber boots with the leg portion under the suite. Judy then taped the bottom of the leg to the boot so no contamination could take place. James put on his gloves next and had his wife tape them to his suit also.

James looked over at David, as he was finishing putting on his suit with his wife's help. David and James were ready to go when James remembered to get a pistol for protection. Both looked at the monitor one more time before they went outside and saw the man still laying on the rock.

James asks, "Judy, please get me a container of water and a little warm soup to give that man outside. Maybe he can drink a little of each without throwing them up. Dr. Rogers, can you fix a syringe of morphine, that I could administer to this man to help him with the pain."

David was picking up the battery charger; the solar cell panel and controller box so the voltage would trickle into the battery correctly. James gave the "ok" to open the big door to Dr. Rogers and Dr. Vickers and the door started to open slowly. David had his mask on and James was putting his mask on as they walked forward.

The view was nothing like when we first went into the shelter. The sky was gray with no clouds and very overcast. The ash was everywhere you looked and James knew they would have to go up to the solar cell on the hill to clean all the ash off the solar cell to make it work properly. As James looked at the man by the rock, James knew the solar cell would have to wait.

David and James walked slowly over to the man and noticed his eyes. They were barely opened a little in order to see us. His face was dirty with mud and had very little clothing on him. James said to him, "I do not know if you can hear me but we are friends and not to be scared, that we are not here to hurt you but to help." David noticed the man was shaking, and asks him "Are you in pain?" He indicated by nodding he was, because his throat was messed up and he could not talk. James informed him, "I am going to give you a morphine shot to help with the pain. When I am done, try to drink some of this hot soup and cool water. Try to rest because we have some work to do." David and James went over to where the metal building was located at and opened the big door. The truck was still there just like they had left if before they went into the shelter. David lifted the hood to get to the battery and James handed him the wires to the charger. Soon as the wires were connected to the battery, we went outside and hooked up the solar panels so the sun could do the charging, if the sun ever comes out. Once that was completed, they knew they were going to have to go back into the shelter soon. As David and James started back to the shelter they noticed the man they talked to a few minutes earlier was laying on his side in the dirt.

James walked over closer to where he was and noticed he was not moving. James then knelt down to take a closer look and then told David, "I think he is dead. We cannot help him now. We need to go inside and wash all this dust off as soon as possible." Both then turned and moved toward the shelter to decontaminate as soon as possible. James started banging on the door for it to open. In a few minutes, the big door started to open slowly. Everyone was glad to see both, James and David, and started the shower of water running to wash the ash and dirt off, so they would not be contaminating inside the shelter.

"The man outside died before we came inside. He was in that bad of condition, like everyone else outside probably will be. I know we feel bad about his death but we need to get ready to be leaving the shelter in about two days.

Martha asked, "What about the man that died outside?"

James said, "He died from being under fed and no water. Judy, I am going to check the radiation outside to be sure that it was low enough for an extended stay, once we go outside. But we can't go until all of our packs are packed with provisions of food, water, and medical supplies. Extra clothes too."

As Judy talked to Bill and Catherine, Betty, Martha, and Sara overheard her say, "Go get some food and fill up your backpacks in order to leave." Betty, Martha, and Sara got the others and started going to the food pantry to fill up their backpack as the children were doing.

James then hollered to everyone, "The food we carry out of the shelter would be all the food we have access to survive on the outside and it will be heavy to carry." After hearing that, it looked like everyone put a couple of extra cans in their packs. Everyone gathered in the big room when they were finished packing.

Sara was the last to come from the medical room. She had helped both Dr. Vickers and Dr. Rogers pack up some medical supplies we would need outside. She quietly stated, "I don't know about the rest of you but I have worked up an appetite. Did we leave anything out for supper?" Everyone laughed.

Betty said, "I started a pot of soup, if anyone is interested."

"Thanks, Betty, we were all packing and didn't think about supper and breakfast in the morning when we leave." James said in an appreciative tone of voice.

"Don't worry James, Judy and Martha and I laid out food for breakfast." Betty said.

"Now that we are all full, and those soup cups have been washed, I am going to lay down for our big day. We are leaving in the a.m.!" Sara responded very loudly.

Chapter Thirteen

Early the next day, the first to wake was Tim. He proceeds to start a pot of coffee as quietly as he can. In the middle of checking out the generator and the cables, James wakes to say, "Good morning, is that coffee I smell."

"Sure is and it will be ready in a few minutes. Just checking out what we need to do to secure the equipment we put in this cave. That way if we or someone else needs to use it, it will be ready. Wish we could take all of it with us. By the way I found some protective suits that are new we can use if necessary? Hey coffee is ready, how you want it?" Tim questioned.

"Black with sugar is fine. These radios and monitors are too heavy to carry and there is no power as far as I know outside. Thanks for getting everything booted up. It is still very dismal looking outside. Thanks, for the coffee, it is perfect. Oh, good morning, ladies. Hope you slept well." James responded to the ladies waking up.

"Sure did, don't know which one of you fixed the coffee, just want to say thanks. Martha, with the generator up and the water already hot it want take long for breakfast to be ready and we can get going." Sara motioned to Martha as she was talking.

"Okay Tim move over and let us gals at the cooking table." Martha said as she prepared the grits, and started the eggs, some scrambled and some boiled while Sara cut up some beef jerky and peanut butter and jelly sandwiches. About that time everyone else was up and ready to go. Dr. Rogers started for a sandwich and boiled egg.

Quickly Sara said "Stop those are for lunch, when we leave today. Get some of the grits and scrambled eggs. Since we are using paper plates and cups so we do not have to do dishes be sure to throw everything down the decontamination waste site at the entrance of the cave. David will we be able to use the pickup truck to put the packs in?"

David said, "I hope so, if the truck will crank."

James then said, "I am going to transmit to the Emergency Management Agency that the radiation was down to about zero and we would be leaving the shelter in a few hours. Be sure to check your suits for tears and small pinholes. We do not want to start out with holes not addressed. If yours is torn in any way, Tim found some new ones that you can use. Preferably use the old one and carry the new ones for later and pin this device on the suit." As James was talking and handing everyone the special protective suits for each of them to put on to protect them from any harmful fallout that may by still out there, James was also handing out a small plastic container.

Before he could finish Catherine questions her dad. "Dad, these suits looked like space suits, with the mask included. Also, what is this device?"

"Those are called Dose meters. They measure the amount of radiation each person absorbs. They have to be read every twenty-four hours. I only have six unites and they must be put on the people that would be most affected by radiation like the children and the thinnest of the rest of us."

"James, we can't forget the guns that the military left us and along with the ammunition that we may need." David reminded James of the weapons. James handed one rifle to David, one to Dr. Vickers, and one to Dr Rogers. The two pistols went to Judy and Sara. About that time, James heard Emergency Management replying on the last transmission he made.

"James Cummings, come in. James, come in. This is Gregg Potter here in Mission Control."

"James Cummings here, go ahead Mission Control. Is this Officer Potter with the Marines?"

"Yes, James. I am glad I was here today to get this message that you are coming out of the cave. Thanks to your information being sent in all the time I only lost a couple of my people that was out there with us. We got back and we did get sick but due to what you did with medical supplies, we got back and survived. Thanks. Good luck. You still going North as you planned. Good luck."

"Thanks, for the update Gregg. Will notify you where we are later if the handheld radios can stay charged with the sunlight. Signing off and shutting down. Tim now you can finish what you started early this morning with the resetting of the equipment. Did you get the codes written down and passed out to everyone? Don't forget the new info on adjustments to the front door that you installed last week. Don't look surprised Martha; if we get separated all of you will know a safe place to return too."

Judy and her children said, "Lets go." With that, everyone got up ready to go outside.

"James I went, rechecked, and found we left some medical supplies that were left in the back room. I am hoping we could add it to the truck. But, I am afraid it might not be enough. Be sure to do as James had instructed us earlier about putting on your mask and making sure your suits are secure. We are limited in medical supplies." Dr. Vickers announced to everyone.

James was about to tell everyone to put their mask on before they go outside to keep from injecting any dust or ash that would be kicked up as they walk.

Betty and Sara said, "Hey we're ready to get out into the sun and fresh air again. Let's go."

David stated, "I hope the sun is showing through the thick overcast air."

Tim, Dr. Vickers, and Dr. Rogers started pulling on the big steel door slowly opening it. James watched as everyone stepped out of the shelter into the fresh air and light. They were shielding their eyes from the bright light that they were not used to for so long. When everyone was outside James started walking over to the man that was slumped over on the rock. The man had not moved at all and James knew he was dead already from the day before.

James turned around, "Tim, help everyone to put their bags in the pickup truck in the metal building. David is opening the door and going to disconnect the charger attached to the battery in order to crank the truck. Before we leave in the truck, I want to take a look at the highway that we came here on and see what shape it is in. Walk with me please Dr. Rogers, and Dr Vickers?" They both nodded okay and started walking toward the hill that was between them and the highway. When they walked over the hill, they could not believe the amount of cars that were piled up on the road. Trees, cars, trucks, and homes and businesses were destroyed or burned up. Human bodies were scattered everywhere.

"How are we going to move anywhere in that mess, is that asphalt twisted up in the road?" Asked David as he walked up behind James and the doctors.

"We need to get back to the rest of our group and get everyone in the truck and get started." James was talking and motioning for the group to get in the truck.

James, Judy, and their two children, Bill and Catherine got in the front and Dr. Rogers, Dr. Vickers got in the second seat, along with Martha Vickers and Betty Goodbye. Tim Guard, David, and Sara Mc Daniel got in the back of the truck with two automatic weapons. When everyone was in the truck, James put the truck in gear and started moving toward the highway.

"Bill, I want you and Catherine to lie down so you want be subjected to what I am seeing in the road." Commanded Judy, their mother. James drove very slowly on the side of the road seeing the dead people lying around everywhere. Most everyone was burned on one side of their body, a few were not burned at all and the rest were shot. It was just a bad situation any way you look at it.

Dr. Ralph Vickers ask, "How far are we going down the road?"

"I think we will get off as soon as we find another good road to get on." James answered. Minutes later Judy hollered, "There is a dirt road just ahead, about one half mile."

James said, "I will take that road to get away from the terrible conditions we are seeing here." After driving a few minutes James turns on the road, "I am going to stop and let Tim, David and Sara get inside the truck. This road is so bumpy and dusty, I am afraid they could fall out the back of the truck, plus it will give us a chance to stretch our legs."

While David and Sara and Tim were rearranging things from the inside of the truck to the back, Tim commented, "I am surprised at how this area has survived everything, there's damage but being it is springtime you can see the new growth on all the foliage that survived. That is a good sign. We are ready to get in the truck, and get going. The windows are up in the back of the truck." James got in his seat and drove about five miles before they spotted a large country house on the left side of the road.

"There's a house just up the road, I think we should stop and make sure everyone is okay." Judy stated. When they arrived at the large house, surrounded by beautiful farmland, a young girl came out on the porch. Judy got out before anyone else could and went up to the girl and started explaining our situation. By the time Judy had finished talking to the young girl everyone was on the porch. In talking, Judy found out the girl was eighteen and had been alone for three months.

Dr. Ralph Vickers asks, "What is your name and where is your family?"

"My name is Sharon Green. My mother, father, and two sisters died for some reason, and I do not know why. I will show you where I dug the graves for them. My family was Amish and did not stay in touch with the outside world very much and we do not even have a radio to play." You could see it in her face how much she missed them.

Dr. Vickers then asks, "Sharon, what were their symptoms before they died?"

Sharon with tears forming in her eyes then stated, "All of them were throwing up a lot, was very red like they were sun burned and was very tired until they died. I tried to give them some water but they only threw up more. I do not know why they died. Excuse me but I cannot help but cry."

Martha Vickers hugged Sharon until she calmed down and said, "My husband will explain what happened to your family."

Dr. Vickers looking Sharon in the eye said, "The United States is now at war and the enemy launched missiles at us with Atomic warheads on them and your family died of radiation poisoning."

"What were they doing before they died?" James asks.

Sharon said, "Everyone was in the field, working the garden and I was in the basement under the house putting up jars of food."

"That is why you did not die; you did not receive the radiation they did while you were staying in the basement." James stated.

Sharon looked so happy when Judy asks, "Sharon, could all of us stay a few days?"

"Yes, I was hoping all of you would, as long as you want to. I have been so lonely for the past few weeks. Come on in and I will fix all of you some food."

James and everyone else were amazed at the variety in food Sharon spread out on the table for them to eat. When fresh sweet potatoes, cream corn, green beans, pickles pears and peaches, homemade gravy over baked chicken, was brought in the room there was complete silence. When Sharon brought out the homemade loaf of bread, Bill and Catherine Cummings looked at each other and shouted in unison "None of us have had bread in a year and it looks delicious."

As everyone sat down to eat, James stated, "Sharon the food looks amazing."

When lunch was over everyone went out to the porch and sat down to talk. A few minutes later Judy said, "Who is that coming down the road?" They saw a girl walking down the dirt road toward the house. Judy, Sara, and Martha went to meet the girl and check to see if she was okay. The girls found she had a black eye and ripped clothes. Everyone could tell that she had been attacked, when the girls reached the house.

Sharon asked, "Where did you come from and what is your name?"

She said, "My name is Betty Anderson from Atlanta, Georgia. My family was attacked, about twenty miles east of here, where my mother, father, and sister were killed by three men wanting food and took anything they could steal."

James asks, "Betty how did you escape the attack?"

Betty said, "I was hit in the face and fell down, then rolled into the bushes before they caught me. One man had a patch over his right eye and he was the one that shot my father."

Bill spoke up, "Someone is walking down the road."

James looked up and saw a man coming toward the house. James picked up the twelve gauge automatic shotgun and started walking toward the man, followed by Betty. When they got closer both James and Betty could tell that the man had a patch over his right eye. James then asks Betty, "Is this the man that has been following you?"

She said, "I do not think so."

When he got closer, Betty said, "Second thought that is the man that killed my father."

James then asks, "Hold the shotgun while I talk to him and get his pistol."

James stopped the man about one hundred yards from the house and asks, "Where are you coming from and what is your name?"

The man replied, "You don't need my name." James heard a huge explosion, as the man, finished replying. James turned to Betty and saw she was shaking and the barrel of the shotgun smoking. James looked back at the man who was now two feet away lying on the ground cut half into, shaking and bleeding everywhere.

Total silence was in the air. Shock affected everybody. No one on the porch could believe what had just happened.

Betty walked slowly to the house and told them, "He will not be killing anyone anymore."

Betty expressed with a firm voice, "James I will not be burying that piece of trash, not after he killed my entire family." James got a shovel and started to go over where the stranger was laying followed by Sharon Green.

James looked at Sharon, "This is what has been happening all over the country for a long time now since the bombs started falling. This is why you should not be alone by yourself. No one has food and will do anything to get some. All of us can help you grow vegetables if you will show us how. We can show you how to defend yourself when the time comes."

After the man was buried, James walked back to the porch, "Judy please drive the truck to the back of the house so we can unload it."

Sharon walked to the back of the house and looked into the back of the truck. "What are in those cans, I do not recognize them."

"It is can food. Why?" Judy questioned.

"I do not recognize can food such as these. The only way I have seen food put up is in jars in the basement. That is the way the Amish has always put up our food."

James explained, "Sharon if you do not farm, you buy food this way. The cans of food are bought at a store. What is further down the dirt road from your house?"

Sharon said, "The only thing I know of is a hardware store owned by an old man and his wife."

James suggested, "Why don't we all drive down to the store and see what he has in stock. We might be able to find some boots to wear when planting the garden with Sharon."

David said, "That is a good idea, I could use some boots."

James asks, "Bill, check the amount of gas we have in the truck, please. Everyone get into the truck."

Bill told his dad, "Dad, the tank is three fourths full and we have three extra cans in the back of the truck."

James said, "Better take those three gas cans out of the back of the truck and hide them by the house. That is the only gas within five hundred miles. Also, make sure the AA Twelves are in the truck, just to be safe."

"What are AA Twelves?" Sharon asks.

James said, "That stands for automatic assault shotguns and generally cannot be owned by the public. The government gave me two in order to protect the underground shelter we have been in recently."

After the cans were hid in the bushes next to the house. Everyone got into the truck and James started driving with Sharon sitting next to him. In about ten minutes, a store next to the road became visible. When we pulled up in front of the store, a middle age man came outside caring a pistol.

"Does everyone carry a gun?" Sharon asked.

"Yes, since the war started everyone is arming themselves with guns of some sort. I don't like it but that is the way it is." Judy stated.

The man asks, "What are you doing here?"

Tim spoke up, "Why we are here is our business." Then the man pulled the trigger of the gun he was holding and shot Tim. The next moment Judy pulled the trigger on the automatic twelve gauge shot gun. The clothing and flesh blasted away from the man's body. Dirt turned to dust and the wood on the house splintered. Judy held her finger on the trigger longer than usual and three rounds fired instead of one. Sharon started to scream and James had to hold her to calm her down.

"I have not seen anything as terrible as that gun in all my life," Sharon still crying but calming down told James.

Bill asks, "Dr. Ralph please check on Tim." Bill, picked up the gun on the ground, put it in his belt, then went over to the man to find he was dead.

Dr. Ralph walked over, checked Tim's pulse, and stated, "Tim is dead."

James said, "Put Tim in the truck, we will bury him back at the house." David started digging a hole to bury the man that was staying at the store while everyone went inside.

Sharon said, "This is not the old man that owned the store for so many years." As they looked around, they noticed the store was almost fully stocked. Everything they needed was there. The boots, shovels, rakes and even matches to their amazement.

James says, "Get what you need but only what you need. We should get some can food if we can find some that has not spoiled."

David hollers, "I found some boots that fit me and some shot gun shells to fit the AA Twelve."

"I will be glad to find something to wear other than these old clothes I am wearing. They are very old and in very bad condition. Hey, Judy, you, and Sara need to look at what I just found. They have blouses and slacks and undergarments for men and women and children," Martha Vickers calls to the other women.

"Dr. Rogers, I just found some medical supplies that are important when needed." Dr. Ralph Vickers stated in surprise. He never dreamed a country store would have surgery supplies.

"Mr. Cummings, I found some different types of food that would be different to eat and some food I have never seen before. I also found some tools to work in the garden, shovels, pick axe, and rakes, and twine to make a trellis for beans to climb on." Sharon proceeded outside to the truck and put what she had in her arms in the truck. Looking around she could not find the grave of the old man that owned the store or his wife anywhere. She knew he was such a nice man the few times she met him.

"Hey, everybody, Sharon beat us back to the truck. Let us put what we found in the back of the truck so we can head back to Sharon's house and warm up some of that delicious food Sharon served us at lunch for supper." James stated.

Betty hollered, "I am still looking for a sun hat to wear while working in the garden." After Betty found the sun hat, she was looking for she picked up more for the others who wanted one. Everyone got into the truck and started back toward the house. We drove about twenty minutes when the house came into view and there were three horses tied in front. Since Judy was driving back, it made it easy for James and David to both pick up a shotgun each. Everyone looked at each other wondering what we were going to do now.

As we drove up two men and a woman came out on the porch. All of us got out when the truck stopped. Sharon stepped up and hollered, "This is my house, and I want to know what are you doing here?"

The woman with the two men said, "We are looking for the man who shot my husband and was looking in the house to see if anybody was inside."

Sharon asks, "What does the man look like?"

The woman said, "He wore a patch over his right eye and was about six feet tall."

Judy then walked up to the woman on the porch, "You will never find him because he is buried under my feet where I shot him."

One of the men asked, "What did the man do to get shot?"

"He shot one of our friends. At least he will not be shooting anyone anymore." Judy said.

James asks, "Is there anything you need before you leave?"

"We could use some water if you could spare some." The woman indicated.

Sharon stated. "I will get you two gallons in just one minute." After receiving the water, the three got on their horses and rode away. James, Sharon, and the rest went inside to get ready for supper. James and David came back out to the truck with two shovels and started digging a grave for Tim who was still lying in the back of the truck.

"This is going to take a while to get this grave deep enough, Dr. Rogers would you say a prayer for Tim." David stated. James and David finished getting things set and everyone came out to give Tim a proper burial before supper was ready.

"Thanks for saying a prayer over a dear friend, Dr. Rogers," Judy remarked.

"The food tonight is as good as it was at lunch." Catherine professed.

"Thanks for the compliment, Catherine. While everyone is eating, I wanted to tell you lay wherever you are comfortable to sleep and I will show you how my parents taught me to plant a garden in the morning. You folks do as you please I am going to bed. Goodnight." As Sharon says goodnight she gets up stretches and goes toward her bedroom.

Chapter Fourteen

The next morning we were in the field planting all kinds of vegetables and the sun hats that Martha found were coming in handy. The new boots we all found were rough on our feet because they were not broke in and were stiff. Everyone was crawling around on their hands and knees to do the planting when Sharon Green said, "Listen, I hear a bunch of horses coming over the hill with riders."

"Better take up the positions we discussed to defend our little group." James noted as he said this, half the group ran to get their weapons and get in position. James, Judy and the rest of the group stayed and kept digging while the riders kept coming. All the riders stopped about twelve feet before they got to the garden. James looked up and said. "Hi folks, hope you have had a good day. Can we help you with anything? Do you need anything special?"

One of the men said, "We need food and water."

Judy spoke up, "Everyone wants something after the war began but we have only enough food to feed ourselves from day to day but we will give you water if that will help."

The man then said, "There is twelve of us and only a few of you crawling around and we could always take what we want."

James then stood up, "We have all of been living underground since the war began and we're use to taking care of ourselves and all I have to do is touch my sunhat and all twelve of you would be shot before you could scratch your ass. The best thing you could do would be to accept the water and continue down the road for about four miles to a general store on the left, where you can get some rakes, shovels and other equipment to plant a garden for yourselves."

Sharon spoke up, "I will give you some seed that you can use. I noticed you have an extra horse you are not using and was wondering if you would consider swapping the horse for some cans of food."

One of the men said, "Sure we will swap the horse we do not need the horse anymore." Then Sharon asks, "James and Judy would you come help me get the food from within my home."

When all three of them were in the house, Sharon stated, "I do not want the men to know where the food is located. Thanks for being here and helping." In a few minutes they walked out with three big boxes of food to give the men on the horses. Then the men handed over the horse to James and Sharon.

Sharon said, "Thanks, the extra horse will be handy to pull the heavy plow in the garden." All the men then started riding down the dirt road to the general store.

Sharon then said, "Better start back working in the garden if everyone wants to eat." David then asks, "Sharon where do you get the water to water the garden?"

Sharon pointed over to the left where a little creek was running through the woods. David and Sharon walked over to the creek and David then ask, "Sharon does the creek come from a lake, where we might catch some fish."

"No," Sharon said, "it comes out of the side of a mountain." David then went and told James what Sharon just said and James just stared at David.

James said, "We just might have ourselves another cave with water." James and David walked over to Sharon and Judy, "We're going to walk up the stream and check it out."

"James, wait just a minute. I want to get some C four explosives to use on the mountain." David remarked.

"David that would be a good idea, because we might need it." James agreeing with David. When David got back from the truck with the explosives he and James started walking up the stream, hoping it wasn't too far.

After about an hour of walking and admiring the countryside, they found the stream flowing out of the side of the mountain about six feet off the ground. James pointed at a position to the side of the mountain and indicated that this would be a good spot to put the explosives and David agreed. David went to work placing the explosives that resembles putty in the rock and placed the igniter charge in the middle of each of them. "This should blow a good size hole for us to get a good look at what we are in for," David said. Both James and David stood back behind a large tree and David pushed the remote control button. The explosion was huge with rocks flying everywhere.

"I am glad we were a long ways away and behind that big tree." James committed. When the smoke and dust cleared, they saw the large hole the explosion had left but had not broken through to a cave if there was one.

"James I am going to have to set a second charge in the back of the hole to get a larger opening to see what is in there." David noticed after saying that to James that James was coming over to help him set the second set of charges in the far back of the hole. The rough and crumbly rock made it hard to walk, work, and work to set the charges. Between James and David, they were able to get the last of the four charges set. Walking back to the same tree David handed James the remote control and said, "You get the honor this time."

James looked at David and smiled saying, "Well here goes nothing." Then there was a second explosion. Rock, dirt, and smoke went everywhere and when James looked around the tree, David could see a big smile on his face. Then David looked and saw a much bigger hole than the first time with an opening in the back that indicated a cave where the water was coming from.

David walked over to the large hole and motioned to James to come on. James was carrying the small flashlight and David carried the large one. Both climbed in the cave with James flashlight on and David following him. "It sure is black in here; my light is not traveling very far. David turn your big light on high, so we can tell how big this cave is?" Light gets brighter and once their eyes adjust, "Wow it is as big as a football field, with huge boulders everywhere." Hollers David, causing the sound to bounce off the cave's boulders.

James then stated, "David, I am getting hungry and am hoping you are ready to get back for supper."

David then said, "I am also ready to go back." Both of them turned to go back to the large entrance of the cave. Getting out of the cave was a job considering all the lose rocks and dirt. When James and David got in the opening James stated, "After being in a black shelter for so long with no fresh air and sunshine I do not think I want to go back in that cave to stay for any time at all."

"I agree with you James." As David agreed, they started walking up stream to get back for some food. Both of them were getting tired after walking for almost two hours.

By the time they got back, everyone had stopped working in the garden and were in the house. When James and David came in the house they found everyone gathered around Judy. Immediately James says, "Move over, what happened to my wife?" James saw her leg was cut deep. James questioned, "How did this happen?"

Bill James son spoke up, "Mom fell on a sharp spade."

"James, I want to inform you that Judy is going to have to have stitches for that cut." Dr. Vickers said calmly trying to calm down James.

James turns and not meaning to snap, "Doc have you got the materials to do the job."

"I do have what I need, except one thing. I need all of you to sit down and stay back. Dr Rogers, I need your help with the procedure to sew up Judy's leg, please. And James you need to put a pillow under your wife's head to make her more comfortable."

Dr. Vickers speaking so firmly it sounded as if he was a General in the service to everyone.

"Judy, I am going to give you a shot to deaden the area, to help with the pain." By the time doc had spoken to Judy, the shot had kicked in and he went immediately to stitching up the leg, which took about thirty minutes.

Judy while lying down and waiting says, "When you going to start Doc, cause I am not feeling a thing."

"Finishing up now, Judy. All's left is to finish taping the wrap around your leg, to keep down infection. Judy, you are not to walk on the leg for the rest of the day. Per my instructions. Do you understand me Judy?" ask Dr. Vickers.

Dr. Rogers spoke up, "Look everyone; we are going to have to be careful from now on. We do not have that much medical to spare. By the way, who is fixing supper?"

Betty Anderson, spoke up and said, "I am, be ready in thirty minutes."

As Betty said, thirty minutes later she hollers, "Come and get it." Everyone sat down and ate a simple supper of potatoes corn and bread before starting to talk about the future.

"I think someone should stay up at night and watch out for any trouble that might be coming our way, to be on the safe side."

Bill said, "Dad, I think that would be a good idea. I would like to be the first to stay up, on a four-hour watch."

Judy stated, "There are a lot of terrible things happening out there, with starvation and other things still happening. We sure do not want to be caught off guard after what we have been through so far."

Bill said, "I will be in the foxhole I dug earlier in the week while goofing off."

"What foxhole?" Bills mother asked.

"While you all were planting the seeds in the garden, I went on the other side of the road and dug down just to see what I could find and it's big enough to hide in, big enough for dad. I will take the hand held radio to call you if I see any one down the dirt road."

"I don't like you doing this, but with what you have helped us with and how you have matured over the last several months, I am going to trust you to call out and stay sharp eyed." Bills mother said with a sad sound in her voice. Everyone agreed and started to bed. Bill started crawling to his foxhole to start his watch. After four hours, Bill was tired and cold and started his way back to the house to wake up his dad for his watch.

When Bill got to the house, he quietly woke up his Dad in a whispering tone, "Dad, it is time for your watch," and handed him the radio. James then got up and put on his coat then got his gun and started his way to the foxhole for his watch that night. James had been in his location for about ten minutes when he heard horses coming down the dirt road with eight men riding in and he immediately called on his radio, "David there's eight men coming on horseback towards all of you."

Earlier after Bill left for the foxhole, before they laid down everyone decided to have stations assigned in the house for safety. They quickly got their coats and guns, and headed to their station.

With everyone in position, James called out to the closest man heading to the house.

"You and your men turn around and head back down the dirt road."

The man hollered and said, "We need food and water and we are not leaving until we get some."

James then told the man, "Okay we can furnish you with water now to drink and some to carry with you. My friends can fix some food to eat now but if you continue, moving toward the house there are twelve automatic weapons pointed at you and I can guarantee that all of you will be killed. There is a hardware store about two miles down the dirt road where you can get other supplies, you need."

The man in front said, "Thanks, we will take the water and food and move on down the road, and we do not want any trouble."

James then asks Judy over the radio, "Judy will you bring out water and food to these men." A few minutes later Judy came out with the water for the men and David came out with the food. All the men got off their horses and sat on the ground to eat. James told everyone over the radio to, "Keep your guns ready if you need to use them." James went over to see what they were eating and found soup and baked potato to be in their lap.

David asks these men sitting on the ground to listen to him: "We know you all have had a hard time over the past months as everyone else had. We all are going to try to make the best of what we have to work with."

After everyone had finished eating James came over to the men; "This is all we have to offer you and you need to move on."

All the men then put their plates down on the ground, got on their horses, and started to ride down the dirt road. Sharon and Betty went out to the yard to collect the plates and began washing them while James made his rounds to check if everyone was on watch like they were instructed to do. About two hours later everyone was getting ready to go back to bed and James ask, "Has any one seen my wife Judy?"

Sara then stated, "I have not seen Judy or your daughter Catherine since the men left earlier tonight."

Sara then saw the color drain out of James face and he became very upset. Sara then said in a very loud voice, "Everyone start searching everywhere for Judy and Catherine quickly. They have to be around here somewhere. If not here, those men on the horses might have taken them," Sara stated, looking at James.

"David how much gas is left in the cans we brought with us?" David looked up at James and said, "I think we have about five gallons left."

"Well that will have to do, David, and Dr. Ralph, Dr. Rogers, let's go after my wife and daughter. The rest of you stay and guard the house until we get back," James stated. All of the men got into the truck with their guns and headed down the dirt road. In about twenty minutes, they saw all the horses outside the hardware store with everyone inside. James drove to about two hundred feet of the house where the car gave out of gas and stopped.

David said, "Well I guess we won't be using this truck anymore."

James said, "Be quiet getting out of the truck and on your way up to the way to the house." When they looked in the windows James saw his wife Judy and daughter Catherine sitting on the floor with their hands tied behind their backs.

David whispered, "Let's go in and get them out." All the men then got their guns and headed into the house. James kicked the door down and opened fire killing all eight men in a split second. When the last shot was fired, James wife Judy looked horrified after all those men were dead. James stated, "No one deserves to live after what they did, when we fed and gave them water. Then they kidnapped you both so they could sell you for food and supplies. How's your leg Judy?"

"It will be okay." Judy remarked.

David mentioned, "Dr. Ralph , Dr. Rogers, we should get back to the big house, to check on our own women folks and make sure they are okay."

Once outside James said, "Well I don't think we will be using the truck to go back to the house."

"We could use the eight horses left outside since the men will not need them anymore." "Good idea, Dr. Ralph, everyone grab a horse and get the reign's of a second one, so we can bring back all eight." As soon as David finished, he heard James ask, "Judy do you think you can ride." Then he heard Judy reply, "Help me up on this brown filly, and I will try not to fall off."

Everyone then got on a horse and started moving toward the big house to check to see if everything is okay.

When they arrived at the house, David found the guards were doing what James asked them to do for protection. James got off his horse and went in to check on everybody and found Betty Goodbye holding her leg with a bloody cloth wrapped around it.

James quizzed Betty "What happened Betty?" Then turned and said "Dr. Vickers, you need to look at Betty's leg to make sure it is okay." Dr Vickers after looking at her leg told, "James Betty's leg will be just fine with a clean bandage."

Judy told everyone, "It was time for them to come to the table for something to eat." After everyone sat down Judy told everyone at the table that "I think we should start helping those roaming around starving and without water. We have food and water, but so many out there do not."

"That can be very dangerous as desperate as everyone is," Betty commented.

James then stated, "I agree, it is time for us to try to help those that are in need. Not everyone is in as good a shape as we are. We will put water and cans of food in the saddle bags on the horses and ride out to find those that are still living and hungry," James commented.

Dr. Vickers stated, "I will put some medical supplies in with the food also."

James then told his son, "Bill please, go feed, and water the horses so they will be ready to ride." Bill went outside to gather the horses and put the bags on them to hold the food and medical supplies. Judy, Sara, and Betty Goodbye then began gathering the food in jars to put in the bags. Everyone then went outside and got on their horses to begin riding.

James said, "Everyone start riding down the dirt road toward the hard ware store. That will be away from the main road where all the death and vileness is."

Martha said, "It's getting late, I think we should get moving." With that being said, all eight of them started going down the dirt road to give help to those who are in need.

After riding about an hour, they saw the hardware store and their old truck, which was out of gas, was still there out in front of the store...

Sara said, "I wonder if there is anything in there we could use?"

Martha hollered, "I am not going in there with all those dead bodies in there."

Sara's husband David said, "Let's continue going down the road so we can do some good." James, Judy, David, and Sara with all the others continued to ride down the road to see if they could find anyone needing their help.

Chapter Fifteen

After a night's rest, the warm morning sun woke Catherine. She proceeded to wake her parents and all of the others. James, Judy, David, Sara, Dr. Ralph, his wife Martha, Dr. Rogers, and his girl friend Betty and Sharon and Betty Anderson all got ready to travel to help those in need.

"I don t like guns but don't forget to pick up your gun just in case someone wants to cause trouble." Betty Anderson said. All of them mounted their horses with some riding two to a saddle and started riding down the dirt road. None of the group knew much about horses much less how to ride them.

After about four hours, Judy stated, "My butt is starting to hurt from the constant bouncing on this horse and I want to get off for a while."

About that time, David saw a shelter, "Dr. Rogers I think someone is living there."

Dr. Rogers stated "I thank you are right". Everyone rode up to the shack and got off their horses the best they could.

David requested, "Don't forget your firearms." James led the way into the front door with everyone else following him. Everyone stopped dead in their tracks from what they were looking at, two men and one woman were shot many times lying on the floor. Their shoes and boots were taken off and their clothes were ripped from top to bottom.

"So this is what this world has turned into," Bill stated.

"I was afraid this is what we would find when we came in the shack. Everybody has gone crazy from hunger and pain," David stated.

Judy was crying holding her hands over her face saying, "At least we should bury them."

After they were buried, Dr. Rogers stated, "Maybe we should ride on in order to check on as many people as possible," I'm sure there are a lot of individuals in desperate need of medical attention and food and water."

Two hours later, the group came upon three women laying under a tree holding out their hands to us, begging us to come over to them. Sara, Judy, and Martha Vickers rode over first in order not to frighten them.

Looking at the women from a distance Betty Anderson said, "You can tell they have been through a lot because they are so dirty with torn clothing." Everyone got off their horses and walked over to the three women who were crying by this time and asking, "Do you have any food at all? James pulled a rabbit leg out of his pocket wrapped in paper and gave it to one of the women, and Judy gave the other two women two baked potatoes to eat.

Martha Vickers started a fire to heat some water to start washing up the women and start some fresh soup to serve because she was sure they were dehydrated by this time.

None of the group took out their guns in order not to upset the women because they had been through enough. Judy, Sara, and Martha Vickers all took some of their clothes and gave them to the women. That was the first smile we saw on their faces since we rode up on the horses.

Everyone put some vegetables in the boiling water to cook so the women could have plenty to eat. One woman did not have a pair of shoes so David's wife Sara gave her a pair to keep her warm.

Dr. Roger and Dr. Vickers went about treating their cuts and bug bites. When the doc's did all they could do; they confided to the women that the group would be moving on to help others in need. The women then begged them if they could come with the group and help because they would most certainly die where they were staying?

Dr. Vickers, our general physician looked at everyone including his wife, Martha and nodded "yes."

The women got on the saddles behind Judy, Sara, and Martha.

Everyone knew riding down the dirt road that this world was once a good place to live and raise a family until different politicians thought starting a war was the best solution to solving their problems.

"We will continue to ride with food and water in order to help people the way we were taught since time began. It is not much but at least it is better than doing nothing." James stated.

Fred Hamlin

www.ingramcontent.com/pod-product-compliance
Lightning Source LLC
Chambersburg PA
CBHW071410170626
46811CB00003B/1344